Dedicated to my dear wife Leonie.

Acknowledgements

I must thank all my family and friends who have encouraged me to start and finish this venture that has been bubbling around in my head for the last three years.

To those who have sown the seeds for a good tale and any who have been witness to the encounters with duppies and supernatural events that are included here for all to share.

To Maas Alvan for his delightful story: The Saintly Duppy.

To Darrel (now deceased), for his information that led to the story about Rollin' Calf and Hoopin' Bwoy.

To Geana whose father told her the frightening tale of Obeah versus Obeah and The Donkey's Revenge.

To my dear Leonie, who was my inspiration and for her stories of The Great Train Crash, The Shroud Pins and The Crocodile Man.

To Pearl, a good friend of Leonie and me, in Nottingham, England for planting the idea for An English Duppy Story.

To Roy (Spoogy) for his never ending humour and his encounter with The Alligator and Trick and a Treat.

To Auntie Winnie (now deceased wife of Alvan) for sharing her face to face experience in Duppy Mellow and the Mangoes.

To Lester for his enthusiasm.

To Fred (deceased) for telling his daughter of a meeting with an adversary in Never Cross A Coolie Man and The Man who Stayed out Late.

To Bertha (deceased) who told of an experience in Duppies on Donkey's Hill to her daughter.

To the roast yam seller for the Boy and the Barble Dove.

To the lady assistant in the Mandeville Public Library, for her courtesy and assistance.

To the National Library of Jamaica in Kingston for their wonderful resources.

To my daughter Marie, for her help with the preliminary typing and word processing.

A special vote of thanks to John Stilgoe for helping the stories come to life with his wonderful illustrations.

Finally, to Mike Henry, my publisher, without whom you would not be reading this book.

Contents

Introduction

You may well ask how it is that a white man, born and bred in Nottingham, England is involved in the searching and writing of stories concerning supernatural incidents in Jamaica.

Well, in 1994 I had the good fortune to meet and marry Leonie (affectionately called Bibby or Nurse by her friends), a Jamaican born woman working and living in Britain. During these last five years of companionship, I have been fascinated by the anecdotal yarns that she has to tell about her life as a child and her home in Porus, Manchester, Jamaica.

I was particularly intrigued by the stories she would relate about the duppies or ghosts, who are prone to wander in the bush, cemeteries and other places of darkness.

She remembers particularly well how her aunt Laura's son Harold, would come to baby-sit herself and her sister Amy (Sissy) when they were six and eight years old respectively, and how he would frighten them at night with supernatural stories, some of which you will find in this book.

Leonie believes that these frightening tales are often told to children for the purpose of keeping them 'in line', by threatening them with all sorts of bogeymen who might come to take them away if they're naughty.

A Jamaican friend said to me recently that "you will find Jamaica to be a nation of devout Church going Christians, but under the surface there lives the 'bush' man, with his myriad superstitions and fears of the unknown, scared of spirits and duppies", so I went to Jamaica, to track the duppies to their haunts, by squeezing out from the people a few interesting stories. Not that I found squeezing necessary, because at the mere mention of a duppy, tales would flow freely and willingly from the family, friends and hospitable strangers who crossed my path.

Many of the narratives are wealthy in imagination, coming as they do from an environment so conducive for their birth.

There was a time when electric lighting was not common in many rural parts of the country, so there were many opportunities for darkness, moonlight, shadow and moving foliage to germinate many an account of inexplicable events, like a tale I was told about two girls who refused to leave their house one night because a duppy was dancing in the yard, to find in the light of day, that it was only a large palm leaf moving in the breeze.

The divulgences were most rewarding, because back in England I was having great difficulty extracting information from many of my Jamaican friends. These senior citizens would claim they had forgotten most of these cultural folk tales. No wonder that the second and third generation in Britain do not receive the mixed blessings of stories that make you pull the sheets over your head at night. This is such a shame, because folklore has such an important part to play in keeping cultural traditions alive.

For some years I spent time in the National Health Service as a drama therapist, which partially involved the therapeutic use of story telling, so I never turn down an opportunity to tell or listen to a good yarn. There are good reasons to keep folklore heritage alive by telling the 'old' stories and recording them for the pleasure of future generations.

This book will endeavour to give you a potpourri of authentic stories, some 'true', some ugly and sinister, some amusing and some created from my own imagination.

Much of this material originates in Porus and the surrounding district of Redberry, Manchester and visits to such locations as Old Harbour in St. Catherine, various fishing villages in Clarendon and Kendal for the Train Crash, amongst others.

I have attempted to reflect the flavour of the stories by holding conversations in Patois, the local dialect of the island. For those unfamiliar with this rich language, translations are in the footnotes.

These 'fire side' tales are presented in the brief, as they were narrated, and I hope that I have been able to capture the essence of these intriguing short stories.

Many of the events and characters in these stories are true, so all names and persons have been changed to protect the innocent.

Please feel free to leave on your night light after you've read this book.

DUPPY

is

derived

from

a

Bantu

language

word

meaning

GHOST

The Duppies on Donkey's Hill

Bibby's mother told her this story when she was a little girl, concerning a frightening episode in her life.

It was when she was a teenager, living on Acre Street, Redberry District, Manchester Parish in the 1920's.

The area was even more densely vegetated than today and it was a time when there was no street lighting and on dark moonlit nights every movement and sound took on fearful interpretations.

This account is accepted amongst the family as a true and actual witness of events that happened.

****

My name is Martha Turbet and I live with my parents on Acre Street in Porus, Manchester, Jamaica. My father John was a butcher at the Porus market, but he was not a well man, suffering with a bad chest. Mother Jane stayed at home as a housewife to look after Anne, Dora, Lena, Jenny and John and myself.

At the age of seventeen I was a higgler and I travelled every day to Mandeville Market to sell fruit and farm produce.

This particular time I arrived home late from a long day, to find that mother had already cooked, everyone had eaten, but nothing was left for me. Mother was like that!

Pappa was very upset about my misfortune, but mamma 'ruled the roost', so all he could do was to sympathise with me, then send me out to tend to the donkey, which my sisters were too 'ladylike' to do. I can well remember the fuss I made, but eventually it was easier to go than to make a useless commotion.

The donkey was tethered to graze some distance away, down the hill from the house, across the gully, then up another hill until we came to the wall surrounding our field. I had grumbled my way down to the gully, crossed over and was starting to climb, when a sound froze me in my tracks. I stood, quite fixed to the spot, as my eyes and ears strained into the dark night for a clue as to the cause. Slowly the night air gave up a sound. The sobbing of a baby. Distant at first but coming closer.

[1]"A wanda who lef dis yah pickney out yah so late?"

I searched around as best I could in the darkness, but no sign of a baby.

"Hush, hush, hush."

The gentle cooing of a mother, whispering to soothe her child drifted down the hill towards me, so I pressed on expecting to meet up with some mother and child crossing our land.

I called out "A who dat?"..... but no reply!

Reaching the donkey I busied myself, talking to the creature and moving its tether to better grazing.

As I climbed the hill back to the house, the baby's crying started again with a vengeance, a pitiful entreaty coming seemingly from everywhere.

Then something came bumpity bumping down the hill.

Two ball-shaped objects were rolling towards me and I only just managed to avoid them, jumping to one side as they shot past and careered into the gully. To my horror I realised that the balls were in fact the heads of two large-eyed infants, uttering most mournful cries of anguish. They were followed by the running spectre of a woman, calling after them ..... "Hush, hush, hush", but they only continued to scream and wail until they passed out of my sight and hearing.

A lady in the district had recently died during the delivery of twins, both of whom died with the mother.

---

[1] "I wonder who's left a baby out here so late?"

The Duppies on Donkey's Hill

My legs hardly carrying me home, I burst sobbing into the kitchen where Mother Jane stood cleaning the pots of the day. Flinging my arms around her, I stuttered and stammered to tell of my fearful experience, at which she began to shout and curse, then pushing me away she ran into the yard, shouting and cussing all around the house. I was told that this was to keep the duppy at bay ..... [2]tarra, tarra, tarra!

I fell into a swoon and could not recall anything for the next three days, pappa telling me later that my fear had thrown me into a fit, with lockjaw and foaming at the mouth. Father had treated me by boiling up cobwebs, feeding the juice to me with a spoon, but it was many days before I returned to my normal self.

****

Some months later, returning home from the market. I was promptly asked to tend our donkey.

In view of my previous experience I was more reluctant than ever to go, but I began this worrying trip, creeping down to the gully with great trepidation, furtively listening and watching for anything untoward.

All went well until I approached the perimeter of the donkey's field, when a glow in the darkness attracted my attention. Crouching down I quietly advanced, to discern a fire on top of the wall. Over the fire was a large iron pot and stirring its contents was the figure of a man I recognised as Chuku.

Now Chuku had been an odd job man, who plied his trade in the local community, but he had died of pneumonia some months back, around the time that the lady and her twins had passed over.

My heart beat as if it would burst, sweat formed in large beads on my forehead and the palms of my hands became clammy and shook uncontrollably. I dropped to the ground, anxious not to be seen and watched this ghostly play unfold.

From the other side of the wall a lady appeared, carrying two

---

[2] A respectable way to swear

5

pickneys in her arms. Placing her babies on the wall, she climbed up beside them, retrieved her young ones and placed one on each breast to feed. Chuku smiled and ladled out the stew, the smell of duppy [3]mussa wafting over to my nostrils as I lay shaking on the ground. Pulling myself together, I edged backward to crawl halfway down the hill, where I sprang up to run like fire, never looking back until I reached the safety of our yard.

Mamma and pappa listened yet again as I told my unbelievable story, but once more before I could finish, Mother Jane was stamping around the house, shouting and cussing enough to arouse the whole district. The poor donkey was not moved that night, and when pappa went to tend it (in daylight of course), the poor creature had grown a film over both eyes.

Until his dying day John blamed the duppies for this affliction to his animal.

I survived, but never went onto the donkey's hill again ..... at night!

---

[3] Mussa is the food of the duppies.

The Legend of Gashanami

This African legend may be the source of stories about 'Rollin' Calf, that are told in Jamaica to this very day.

This creature is an unpleasant ghostly black bull that seems to enjoy following and terrifying its victims when they are unfortunate enough to be caught out late at night. He is likely to confront you on some lonely moonlit road in the bush, where he will stand with eyes dripping fire, shaking his enormous horns and striking sparks as he paws the ground. Around his neck there will probably be a rattling chain; not that one should endeavour to check this out, because if you touch him you will surely die. It is said, however, that if you defeat this bull in mortal combat, you will live forever, but there have been no claims so far for this Lonsdale belt of life everlasting. This Jamaican calf is only a servant to the original African bull Gashanami, the God of Vengeance, who had the ability to grow to enormous size at will. An encounter with any member of this bovine family, however, is to be discouraged, because folks go missing after they cross the path of these mad bulls.

The favourite haunt of the calves of our ' terror bull' seems to have been in the rugged Cockpit country in Trelawny, but I am sure that they get around quite a bit. There may very well be numerous calves from Gashanami, because it is said that murderers and butchers become Rollin' Calves when they leave this mortal toil. Or do you think it's true that plantation owners made up the legend and passed it around, to stop the slaves from wandering at night?

* * * * * * *

Gashanami bellowed out his terrifying challenge to the surrounding countryside. This gigantic bull stood, a magnificent sight, his fiery eyes surveying the valley below, where he had been on the rampage with his calves, bringing terror to the surrounding villages, slaughtering all that stood in their path, for no-one ever survived such an encounter.

The villagers were so afraid that most were staying close by their huts, where they hoped that they would be safe from this orgy of bloodshed. All that is, except a beautiful maiden of the tribe, who seemed to be immune to the dread that was seeping through the community. She was in need of a clean garment, so collecting her washing materials together, she left the circle of huts and headed for the river. It was a warm day and she sang as she rubbed and beat her dress on the large now smooth stone that sat close by the water. So engrossed was she in her labour, that she failed to notice the strange stillness that was falling all around. Bending over the river's edge to rinse her apparel, she was startled by the reflection of some large creature that stood behind her and spinning round, she found herself looking directly into the red eyes of the mighty bull.

Dropping her laundry, she sprang to one side to escape this monstrosity, but to no avail, for Gashanami lunged forward and the screaming girl was impaled on one of its enormous horns. He tossed her about in the air like some old discarded rag doll, before flinging her gory corpse up into a nearby tree, where it hung and bled until she was found by a horrified party of villagers the following day.

It was wailing and gnashing of teeth at the funeral of yet another victim of this duppy beast and all was despair for the future, when a warrior leapt to his feet, shook his fists to the heavens and cried out for revenge:

"Who will follow me into the forest to slay our oppressor?"

It was Quoa, son of the chieftain, a favoured fighter amongst the young men of the tribe. Everyone turned away in shame, for none of his people had the courage to face their worst fear. Undeterred, Quoa took up his trusted axe and left the cowardly village, determined to take his own personal vengeance to the god.

Starting at the river bank, he located the spoor of the murderous animal and began his relentless mission to find and strike it dead. He soon became aware that he was on the right track, because he followed the gigantic footprints to devastated bush land and the remains of unfortunate animals, who had been unlucky enough to meet up with Gashanami.

Hearing an enormous disturbance ahead, our prince climbed high up into a giant Cotton Wood tree, wedged himself securely in a branch fork and began to sing:

"Gashanami! You killed my mother, but you can't kill me!"
Over and over he dared the bull to mortal combat.
"Gashanami! You killed my sister, but you can't kill me!"

The terror of the bush replied with a stupendous roar, lumbering at the tree, snorting from smoke filled nostrils and clanking its weighty chain.

Crash! The bull struck the tree a shuddering blow, causing Quoa to cling tightly to his protector.

"Gashanami! You killed my brother, but you can't kill me!"

The bull doubled in size and rushed at the trunk of the Cotton tree with a resounding thud that shook it to its very roots, but our mighty denizen of the forest held firm. Once again the duppy grew to even more monstrous proportions and the duel between two of nature's giants waged for hour after frightening hour, until the relentless slamming by the massive head slowly began to take its toll. The white trunk started to yield and bend under the constant bombardment. Over and over it leaned until its clinging occupant was coming dangerously close to Gashanami's blooded horns, so our brave warrior sang once again:

"I see dry trees fall, but green trees, never!
So bear up for me now, bear up for ever!"

It almost appeared as if the heroic tree shook itself, then groaning and creaking it slowly raised its head, to stand once again, tall and proud amongst its neighbours. So this marathon battle between Gashanami, the Cotton Wood tree, Quoa and magic waged for two whole days and two seemingly endless nights. On the morning of the third day, Gashanami was exhausted and unable to match the magical chanting of Quoa, so he lay down to gather his breath, falling into a deep weary sleep. This was the moment of victory, as Quoa slithered down from the tree, raised his patient axe and delivered a death blow to the huge terror of the forest.

* * * * * * *

Quoa is now eternal, but where are the calf followers of the God of Vengeance? Seeking their revenge in the wild places of Jamaica, that's for sure!

Six Feet Under

This is a story that springs from the author's imagination which could have happened at any place in Jamaica.

It takes place back in the days when the deceased were not placed within fancy sepulchres as they are today, but were buried in good old fashioned holes in the ground.

****

Claudette lay in her coffin in the parlour. She had spent all day, quite still, as her family, friends and neighbours sat or stood around to view her remains. If only she could have joined in the gossip that flowed back and forth.

The undertaker had dressed Claudette beautifully in her white wedding gown and had managed to give her corpse a semblance of a smile.

Tomorrow, she would be six feet under.

****

The grave digger had toiled all day and he also had pride in his work.

As he dug, spadeful by spadeful, he took great care to ensure that the hole was exactly six feet long, by three feet wide and a good six feet deep. The sides were perfectly vertical, to allow for easy passage of the coffin down to the carefully cut floor below.

Today's task had been particularly difficult due to regular downpourings of heavy rain. The soil was sodden with water and threatened to collapse at the slightest touch, but Jonathan knew

11

his craft well, so as he carefully clambered up the small ladder to the surface, he was well pleased.

Pulling the ladder up, glancing down for a final inspection, then slinging the ladder across his shoulder he set off home for some well earned [1]mannish water.

****

The local bar was not well patronised that night as many of the regulars were at Claudette's set up or wake. In fact, if it wasn't for John and Lloyd sitting at a table in the corner, Charlie's Tavern would have been empty.

John and Lloyd were old pals, going back a long way, frequently seen in the bar, drinking and solving the problems of the world. The bar-tender was always happy to see them, for these customers certainly knew in which direction beer and rum was intended to travel.....down the hatch!

John was paying for the drinks, having sold a dining table and four good chairs at his joinery shop that very morning and Lloyd was happy to share the windfall. They both had many a tot since five o'clock and Lloyd was 'well away' by closing time.

'One for the road' had been one too many for John, for he was slumped over the table overwhelmed by alcohol, snoring loud enough to waken the dead.

Lloyd struggled to his feet, tapped his friend affectionately on the head, staggering towards the blur that was the door, choosing the middle one of the three he leant for a moment on the frame to gather himself for the journey ahead.

A lunge got him underway, weaving to and fro down the road, pausing only to give his urgent bladder some relief behind a lignum vitae tree. Back on track, he spent some time failing to prove that the shortest distance between two points is a straight line and he laughed from time to time, as some amusing thought fleeted across the mists of his stuporous mind.

---

[1] Mannish water is a soup made with a goat's head, its tripe and its private parts. It's very tasty.

12

Oh good! Here's the cemetery.

Lloyd leant against the gate, which resisted for a moment, then swung reluctantly open, its rusted hinges uttering a long groan.

This short-cut home was often navigated by him during day light hours, but this route wouldn't be considered during such a dark night if he had been sober enough to take fright at the scuttlings and scrapings of Lord knows what. In the misty darkness Lloyd left the beaten track and stumbled from tomb stone to tomb stone.

Then the world opened under his feet.

He plummeted down, falling with a heavy thud on wet yielding ground, the breath knocked out of him. His relaxed boozy state had protected him from serious injury, but he remained prostrate for some time. Eyes opening reluctantly to the pitch blackness all around, he rolled over onto his back, peered up to the sky, discerning the outline of the hole above.

[2] "Lawd, me inna waan grave!"

His torpid mind came flashing back to sober life.

Letting out a long scream like a [3] Banshee's wail, Lloyd leapt to his feet, ran two steps and flung himself upwards towards the lip of the grave, grasping wildly for a grip to haul himself to safety. All he found was yielding wet soil that fell down onto him as he tumbled backwards.

[4] "Lawd, elp mi!" was the cry, as fear grasped him by the throat.

Time and time again he sprang to the skies, but always with the same result, so he lay sobbing, covered head to foot with wet clingy soil.

As suddenly as it came, his terror broke.

He saw himself, a sweating mass, crouching pitifully at the bottom of this nightmare, so his mind began to reason.

[5] "If mi a gwann wi dis mi go bury misef."

---

[2] "Lord, I'm in a grave!"
[3] An Irish or Scottish female spirit whose wail outside is believed to portend death within.
[4] "Lord, help me!"
[5] "If I carry on like this, I'm going to bury myself."

13

Crying for help was to no avail, as nobody would be coming this way on such a black night, so with a shrug of resignation, he realised that all he could do was to wait until the light of day, or heaven forbid, wait for the funeral party.

Yes! He knew now that he had fallen into Claudette's newly dug grave.

Feeling around for the driest spot, he slumped down to lean on the wall and prepare for a long vigil. Sleep slowly crept up to release him from the discomfort of this terrible situation.

****

A vibrating thud disturbed his sobering slumber.

Lloyd had no idea how much time had elapsed, but it was still dark when his rest was roughly broken. He shook his head, blinked and as his vision adjusted to the gloomy surroundings he saw, lying with his face to the ground, the figure of a man.

****

John had slept solidly for two hours.

To Charlie, the bar was his home, so he was in no hurry to disturb his customer, but just left him to hibernate.

John stirred, shivered and half awoke.

[6] "Gwaan a yu yaad, John."

Still not fully compos mentis, he struggled from the bar.

[7] "Wait fi mi Liedy, mek yu a walk so fast an a lef mi man?"

Calling from time to time, he followed in Lloyd's footsteps and well I never!

He fell right into the grave!

****

---

[6] "Go home John."
[7] "Wait for me Lloyd. Why have you walked so fast and left me man?"

Six Feet Under

Lloyd sat quietly watching the scene unfold as John lived his own episode of terror. John stirred, turned over, screamed and began the futile scramble to get clear of the black hole. He was in a frightening state of hysteria, screaming for God to help him as he tried, over and over, to escape. Realisation of the predicament didn't dawn as it had with Lloyd and he sobbed and pleaded for rescue, shaking in abject fear.

[8] "Im wi ab a 'art attack," thought Lloyd, so he laboriously rose to his feet and took the few steps to his distressed companion. Gently tapping him on the shoulder he said:

[9] "Yuh naa mek hi out yah."

BUT HE DID .....!!

With a howl the wretched man leapt up like an Olympic high jumper, as a sudden surge of adrenaline sent him soaring into the air, to land in a heap by the graveside. Springing up, he ran the hundred yards dash in ten seconds flat, never stopping until he reached his yard, whooping and hollering all the way.

****

For many months to come John told the tale of the night in the graveyard when he had a fearful encounter with a duppy.

Lloyd never enlightened him!!!

---

[8] "He will have a heart attack."
[9] "You won't get out of here."

The Shroud Pins

This is a story told to Leonie by the old folks when she was a girl. It could have happened in many a location in Jamaica.

****

It was still dark as Joshua hitched up his donkey to the old cart. He had been up and about for some time, loading up the cart with his home grown fruit and vegetables, which he sold each week at the market in Mandeville. He needed to start early, so that he could be amongst the first of the higglers to arrive, set up his spot, be ready for the long day ahead and attract buyers from amongst the bustling crowd.

Joshua had to do this alone since his dear wife died a year ago, working hard to eke out a meagre living to support his family.

"Rosanne...! Pearl...! Blossom...!" he called to arouse his three daughters to start on their household chores before their long walk to school.

A feeble response issued from somewhere at the back of the house.

"Giddup!"

Hickie felt the prod of a stick on his rump, so he set off up the track that he knew so well. He did this journey every week and had done so since the day he had been purchased from Brownie, Joshua's neighbour. Hickie was so familiar with the route that Joshua would often be seen dozing away, reins hanging loose, confident that his donkey would take them safely to their destination.

The Shroud Pins

****

It had been a long, hot day and Joshua was tired and looking forward to journeying home. Trade had been brisk, so there was very little produce to reload. Hickie set off at a good trot, being well aware that the day would soon be over. [1]"Cari mi ackee go dung Linstead Markit nat a quatti wot sell." Joshua sang, occasionally shaking the reins and tapping Hickie gently with the cane. He was contented.

Darkness was rapidly drawing in again and Hickie was slowly forgetting his first flush of enthusiasm, his pace now down to ambling. Tiredness crept up on Joshua and he dozed. His heavy eyes started to close and his head sank to his chest, nodding up and down as he struggled to stay awake.

Suddenly! ..... a tall dark figure stepped out in their path. Hickie shied away.

[2]"Ah wah dat?" Joshua awoke with a startled cry, and dropped his stick. His heart was racing and beads of sweat fell from his brow. He looked around furtively and there was no doubt about it; he was scared. His mother's voice came to him saying [3]"No mek nite ketch yu outa doah."

He shook himself and for a fleeting moment a smile crossed his face.

[4] "Duppy agen mamma? Always a frighten mi bout duppy inna bush a nite!"

He stepped down from the cart, bending to retrieve his stick, but quickly started back at the sight of a pair of black boots standing but a step away. Dropping to his knees with shock, his eyes looked up, passing long black trousers, a black jacket and finally a black wide-brimmed hat sitting on top of an ashen black face. How expressionless this face, with doleful eyes staring down at him as he knelt in the dirt. Using the stick for support, Joshua

---

[1] "Carry my ackee (a local vegetable) to Linstead Market, not a pennyworth was sold."
[2] "What's that?"
[3] "Don't be caught out of doors at night-time."
[4] "Ghosts again mother? Always frightening me about ghosts in the woods at night."

slowly arose, brushing his trouser knees, but unable to help stepping back from the stranger.

[5] "Yu frighten mi bad man."

The dark stranger made no response, but stood quite still in the roadway.

Joshua eyed him up and down to see whether he was to be robbed of his day's takings, but the figure remained unmoved, so Joshua racked his brain to guess the reason for this man stopping him on the road.

[6] "Yu laas man? A weh yuh a go?"

Again no reply was forthcoming.

[7] "Yu waan a lif man?"

With head down and stooping back, the figure shuffled to the cart side away from Joshua and with a low sigh, clambered aboard and sat with dangly legs nearly touching the floor.

[8] "Nat eben tanks mi no get" thought Joshua, but with a shrug of his shoulders, he stepped up onto the cart and prodded the donkey into life. Hickie did not seem too anxious to move at first, but eventually a good crack on the back set him off at a fair trot. Joshua thought to set up conversation with the stranger, but never a word could he coax from him.

Home was drawing near when it started to rain as though a giant had emptied his bath from the heavens. You know how it can rain in Jamaica!

Joshua quickly drove into the yard, leapt down , loosened Hickie and dashed to his veranda. Looking back he saw the stranger, unmoved, sitting silently in the rain.

[9] "Cum outa de rain man. Yu wi ketch cole."

Obeying, he slumped from the cart, shuffled slowly to the house, paying no heed of the rain which plummeted down, soaking him through. When he reached the steps to the porch, he just stood there gazing balefully at the house.

[10] "Cum in man." Our higgler was getting a little irate.

---

[5] "You gave me a bad fright man."
[6] "Are you lost man? Where are you going?"
[7] "Do you want a lift man?"
[8] "I don't even get a thank you."

[9] "Come out of the rain man. You'll catch a cold."
[10] "Come in man."

[11] "Tank yu, Sa."

The visitor spoke for the first time in a deep voice that echoed around the yard. His step by weary step to reach the veranda seemed to take a lifetime.

[12] "Cum! Quick! Tek off yu wet cloas. Yu cyaan go no furda like dat."

"Tank yu, Sa," responded the man in black, who duly took off his black wide-brimmed hat and laid it down on the wooden floor.

Took off his black jacket and laid it down on the wooden floor beside his black wide-brimmed hat.

Took off his heavy black boots and laid them down on the wooden floor, beside the black wide-brimmed hat and the black jacket.

He slipped off his long black trousers and laid them down on the wooden floor beside the black wide-brimmed hat and the black jacket and the heavy black boots, and there he stood in a long white garment.

[13] "Yu afi elp mi now Sa!"

[14] "Elp yu! Wah yu waant me fi do fi yu?"

[15] "Mi cyaan pull out di pin dem."

[16] "Pin! Weh yu a taak 'bout?"

[17] "Wah! di SHROUD pin mi mean."

Joshua leapt back in horror as he realised the implication of the words, but before he could rally his shaking legs to carry him away, he became aware that the stranger was smiling at him ... a wry smile!

Joshua was transfixed as the white shrouded visitor slowly lost his features, fading away to leave only the vestige of the smile, a smile that was forever to haunt Joshua, reminding him of his encounter with a duppy.

---

[11] "Thank you, sir."
[12] "Come. Quickly. Take off your wet clothes. You can't go any further like that."
[13] "You will have to help me now sir."
[14] "Help you? What do you want me to do for you?"
[15] "I can't pull out the pins."
[16] "Pins! What are you talking about?"
[17] "Why! I mean the shroud pins."

Did You Know? (1)

That duppies live in Cotton trees.

Seldom, if ever, are these giants of the forest felled without an offering of white rum, rice and the slaying of a rooster. There are those unbelievers who suggest that this legend was fostered by the professional lumberjacks, who claimed the offering for themselves.

* * * * * * *

That the hooting of an owl is a bad omen in Jamaica. If one screeches over your dwelling, it is a sure portent of a forthcoming death in your family. This belief is similar to the Irish tales of 'banshees', those female spirits of the fairies, whose wailing outside of a house is also the sign of an impending demise. I am sure that every nation has stories of such harbingers of death.

* * * * * * *

That duppies like to play with babies.

If they do, the infants are likely to suffer with 'fits' and in later life these evil spirits may sneak the young child away.

* * * * * * *

That if you throw stones at the carrion bird called John Crow, your clothes will tear.

* * * * * * *

That you must clean your shoes before returning home from a funeral.

If you come back to your yard with the dirt from a cemetery

on your shoes, the duppies will surely come to take it back. In any case, clean shoes or not, when returning from anywhere at night, the duppies will try to follow you home. The only way to confuse them is to stop off somewhere to break your journey and this will throw them off the track. If this doesn't deter them, stay outside of your house for a while before going in, for they will become impatient and return to the graveyard.

* * * * * * *

Obeah practitioners can turn duppies into snakes, frogs or lizards.

These can then be sent to 'spit' on a chosen victim, to bring about fevers, bad knees or 'false bellies'(tumours). 'False bellies' are also called 'ten penny bellies'.

* * * * * * *

That duppies like to 'trouble' the bath water of babies.

If you leave your baby's bath water out in the sun to warm, it will surely be a target for mischievous ghosts. To prevent them getting to the water, place two sticks across the basin in the shape of a X. This of course, is the roman numeral for ten and as everyone knows, duppies can only count to nine. To solve the puzzle, they will count, one, two, three and so on to nine and being unable to find ten they will start over again. One, two, three, etc. Eventually they become so frustrated, that they will leave, muttering under their breath all the way back to the graveyard.

* * * * * * *

That whilst you are bathing the baby, add 'blue' (a clothes whitener) to the water and whilst the infant is on your lap, place a drop in the infant's mouth, then a drop on baby's arm, its loins, its buttocks, its ankle and finally its instep. The duppies will not like this one bit.

The Donkey's Revenge

This tale was told by the father of Geana, my wife's hairdresser in Nottingham, England.

This is one of two good tales related to my wife and I, during a visit by our hairdresser and friend, Geana Wallace, a beautiful young lady fortunate enough to have a father who keeps these excellent stories alive, by narrating them to his family.

Mother and father Wallace both originate from a district in Clarendon, and Geana said that pappa could tell duppy stories all night long. I am hoping that more will be forthcoming. Congratulations Mr. Wallace, for having brought up your daughter with a sprinkling of the 'old stories'. You can rest assured that she is keeping them alive 'cos she does tell 'em well!!

****

Aunt B had this donkey, a young donkey.

She constantly complained to her husband and anyone else who would listen, that the donkey was lazy and that it didn't earn its keep.

Poor donkey!

Aunt B would often give it a lickin' with a stick, then would tie it up at the side of the house, so that it couldn't graze and feed. All the donkey could do was to stand there, blink its big brown eyes and noisily flap its large ears, to endure long hours without feed and water.

The husband would work in the fields, cultivating sugar cane that would soon be ready for harvesting and delivering to the local sugar cane factory.

Aunt B continued to nag about her donkey, and told her husband to be sure that it carried full loads of cane to the factory. We know that she meant 'more' than full loads, don't we? I wonder why she wanted to torment this poor creature so?

Our farmer was not as cruel as his wife, however, because when he came down from the fields on Guava Hill after a hard day's labour, he would see to the animal, watering it and giving it feed, but he always left the donkey fastened to the porch rail so as not to draw down the wrath of Aunt B. Still he did treat it better than his wife.

So the donkey would stand there, blinking its big brown eyes and noisily flapping its large ears.

One morning it was time for cutting the cane and transporting it ready for processing. The donkey was untied from the rail; it dutifully followed its master up the hill, glad to stretch its legs, to where the farmer cut the cane and stacked it ready to load.

[1] "Yu mus mek de donkey work 'ard!" Aunt B couldn't resist a comment.

The farmer sighed and raised a hand of acknowledgement.

Loading up the cane .... a fair load ....the farmer talked to his animal, reminding it of the journey ahead and giving a promise of a good feed at the end of the day. Then they set off out of the field and picked their way carefully down the track that led past the house to the main drag below.

Aunt B couldn't resist running out, cane in hand, to give the poor jackass a sharp crack on the rump, followed by a few well chosen words of derision.

They had just stepped down onto the main road, when out of nowhere, a lorry came and knocked the donkey down. The poor creature wasn't killed outright, but it was obviously in pain, suffering close to death.

Aunt B came shouting and bellowing:

[2] "Git up, yu lazy ting," and she made to hit it with her stick.

[3] "Shut up woman. Yu nu si im a ded."

---

[1] "You must make the donkey work hard!"
[2] "Get up you lazy thing."
[3] "Shut up woman. Can't you see that he's near to death."

The Donkey's Revenge

The farmer took his machete and with an apology to his animal, put it out of its misery.

The cane was unloaded.

****

Three weeks later our farmer woke up with a start. Something had disturbed his sleep and he lay, quite still, listening .... listening.

Then from the yard he heard a sound. He recognised it, but couldn't quite place it. The noise was so persistent and got louder and louder until he was quite unable to sleep and had to rise to investigate.

He crept from the bedroom, taking down the kerosene lamp from the wall, struck a light, lit up and tiptoed down the passage. He slowly opened the door, holding the lamp up high as he peered out onto his yard.

What did he see?

Well! Very little really, except a pair of blinking brown eyes which seemed to float suspended in the air.

The sound became clear now. It was the flap flap flapping of a large pair of ears. He couldn't see his donkey, but he knew it was there, because the piece of rope that normally tethered it to the porch, was swinging back and forth, back and forth.

Night after night, week after week, his restive sleep would be disturbed by the flapping of a donkey's ears ..... but no donkey!

****

Two months later, Aunt B, walking along the main road, having been out to buy some fish for supper, approached the house. Night was falling, so the farmer's wife was hurrying home as she didn't like to be caught out in the dark.

Suddenly, from around the back of the house, a dark form careered into view, hooves flying and tail swishing behind. Dark brown eyes flashed in the moonlight. It was a donkey, charging straight towards Aunt B, who backed off, screaming for help.

Thud!

The bristly head struck her full in the chest and with a sharp cry of pain she flew high into the air, her newly bought fish scattering in all directions. She came down to earth with a mighty crash and lay writhing on the ground in pain, but she didn't linger long, fearing that she would be trampled under foot by this mad creature. Rising to her feet, she looked around, wide eyed with fright.

There was no donkey to be seen.

Nursing her cuts and bruises Aunt B told her tale of woe to her husband that night .....

..... but he only smiled!

Never Cross A Coolie Man

The integrated population of Indians now living in Jamaica have an interesting history.

Unlike the Afro-Caribbean population, they didn't arrive on the island as slaves, but as indentured workers. To be indentured was to take on a formal sealed agreement, very much like one that binds an apprentice to a master.

In 1845 two ship loads from India brought workers to British Guyana, Trinidad and Jamaica, with a promise of large numbers to follow, but Jamaica cancelled her outstanding order of Indian immigrants in 1846, pulling out of the scheme on financial grounds due to falling sugar prices. Later as the industry recovered the scheme took on a renewed attraction.

Many of the descendants still live in the Sugar Cane Belt, such as Vere in Clarendon and Frome in Westmoreland.

They came to be called Coolie-men, possibly because of the connections with the Kuli tribesmen of India. This term is not to be confused with the European use of the word Coolie, which denotes Chinamen.

Although considered rude to address Indians in this way, it was widely used in the country areas of Jamaica at the time of this tale.

****

This is a frighteningly true account of an event that took place before I was born and tells of a time when my father was taken critically ill.

****

Pappa has earned his living in many ways.

As a ganger on the Jamaican Railways, he has sawed timber in his own yard, worked as a farmer; has been employed at the bauxite mine where he was a Union Official, but now he was working for a fishery with four other men.

This particular Sunday evening they met and began their familiar walk from Porus to Lionel Town and then on to Rocky Point. Sometimes they went to Milk River or wherever, to take the boat and seek the fish.

As they walked and talked, they came upon a lost puppy standing on the road. Not wanting the tiny thing to starve or be killed on the road, the fishermen decided to carry it with them to make it their lucky mascot.

A mile further down the road they came upon a Coolie man (or as some would say an Indian man), who approached them saying:

[1] "Unu si one puppy out ya?"

All shaking heads, they walked on.

A little while later the Indian man caught up with them again, asking if they'd seen his puppy.

"No", was the reply, with the small puppy still hidden inside a coat.

[2] "Mek mi tell yu sinting. If any a yu tek mi puppy, dem ded. Dis ya sinting mi ab ina mi'an, lickle a it ina yu backside."

With this remark, it was clear that the Coolie man was a practitioner of Obeah, a caster of spells and other such superstitious magic. They supposedly rebuke enveloping forces, resolve love problems and problems with the boss at work, reverse bad luck, return your husband to your home if he leaves you, and a whole heap of other things.

As soon as the Indian man walked off, one of the fishermen told my father Alex that he didn't feel well. It was usual for them to sleep overnight on the boat, but when Alex looked at his friend and realised that he indeed didn't look at all well, he suggested

---

[1] "Have you seen a puppy round here?"

[2] "Let me tell you something. If any of you have taken my puppy, you're dead. Something I have in my hand will soon be up your backside."

that they find the first available shelter. They came across a piazza and settled down as best they could.

The following morning their ailing comrade was looking terrible, laid on his side, his face all twisted and mouth water dribbling down across his cheek to his ear and obviously running a high temperature. They had to find a sympathetic farmer who agreed to take him home on his dray and to call for a doctor.

The four remaining men took the puppy to sea, but soon another of the crew was showing symptoms of the fever that had struck. They set off for the shore, but before making land, their friend was dead.

It was strange that they didn't see the connection between the death, the illness, the puppy and the Obeah man.

They were paid, what little it was, and they set off home, taking the corpse with them on an improvised stretcher.

As they travelled, they crossed the path of the Coolie man again, who pointed his finger at them and said in a cackling voice:
[3] "Mi a waan yu."

This frightened them, got them thinking and talking, and deciding that the puppy was the source of their ailments. So they killed the innocent puppy and threw it away.

It was, of course, the Obeah man who was responsible, because in Jamaica the Indian man has a reputation of making the most powerful magic. Many were afraid of them, so it wasn't surprising that when they reached home, they were informed that the first friend brought back by the farmer was dead, and by this time all three survivors were showing signs of being ill.

My grandmother took Alex in and put him straight to bed, realising how serious was the illness. Father became so ill that he started to see people around the house. Today, we would say that he was hallucinating, but in those days they knew it was the duppies.

He told his mother they were beckoning to him and he had a strong urge to go with them.
[4] "A weh yu a go?" said grandma.

---

[3] "I did warn you!"
[4] "Where are you going?"

31

Never Cross a Coolie Man

[5] "De man dem a caal mi."

[6] "Go bak a yu bed. Yu delireous. Yu fren dem ded. Yu waan ded too?"

[7] "Cum ya mamma."

His mamma joined him at the doorway.

[8] "Luk pan mi grave."

She could see nothing.

[9] "Cum bak, yu sick."

The house was an old colonial type house with a bedroom either end, a large hall in the middle, a veranda all the way around, and a door at each end of the hall. Alex staggered through to the other door, but the grave was there as well.

[10] "The duppy dem cum fi kill mi."

By this time father was in a really bad state, sweating profusely, his eyes protruding and rolling, showing whites with fear. He was punching the air with his fists, as though fighting an invisible assailant and howling like a dog at its master's death bed.

The neighbours told grandma to fetch the Obeah man who lived over the hill, so she raised up her skirt and ran all the way as fast as her feet would carry her. She gasped out her story, but after a long pause the Obeah man advised that it may be too late as he had heard that all the men who went with Alex had taken sick and died.

All this time Alex was subjected to the siren cries of duppies calling him to go with them.

The Obeah man spent some time considering the case, then quickly turned his hand to preparing a lotion.

Grandma ran the mile back home to find her son wandering aimlessly about the yard. She had quite a fight to lead him back into the house, but with help from the neighbours held him down on his bed to sprinkle and rub him all over with the charm lotion.

---

[5] "The men are calling me."

[6] "Go back to your bed. You're delirious. Your friends are dead. Do you want to be dead too?"

[7] "Come here Mama."

[8] "Look upon my grave."

[9] "Come back, you're sick."

[10] "The duppies are coming to kill me."

Alex was then locked in his room, the windows fastened down, the doors bolted shut and every effort made to prevent these malevolent spirits entering the house.

What a night!

How the duppies got the cooking pots into the yard we'll never know, but they bashed and crashed, rattled and clanked right through until morning. Grandma could hear the shingles being torn off the roof, to be cast down into the yard.

It was only when the sun began to appear that the clatter slowly subsided, everything becoming still and strangely silent.

My grandma went apprehensively into the yard, to find that everything was as it should be. Not a shingle was missing and all the pans were in their proper places, apparently undisturbed in the kitchen.

Pappa was still quite ill, but his fever had broken and although he remained weak for many days, he lived to father me ..... and tell me this tale!

Dead, But He Won't Lie Down

This is an imaginary tale that could have taken place at your local cemetery.

****

"Abide with me, fast falls the eventide
The darkness deepens, Lord ....."

The strains of this beloved hymn rang around the wooden walls of the church.

The coffin sat before the lectern.

Arthur's hand-carved benches were filled to capacity, to mourn and celebrate the passing of a dear friend and father.

The minister was in particularly good form, rousing his congregation to fervent amens and alleluias, so that the crying and hollering was indeed praiseworthy.

The men all sat in their best Sunday suits, shirts and ties, obviously in some discomfort due to the oppressively humid and hot weather. Black and white dresses were the order of the day and some ladies, bedecked in their large Sunday hats, wiped the beads of sweat from glistening black foreheads, breezing themselves with large straw fans. The eulogies had lasted for a good hour and a half, as relative after relative, friend after friend had risen to extol the virtues of their dear departed.

The service was coming to an end and the Minister gave clear instruction for the orderly exit to the burial ground. The pall bearers assembled, heaved the coffin to shoulders and led the way down the aisle, followed closely by the Minister, Bible in hand. Weeping relatives took their place in procession and then the body of the congregation fell into line, to wend its way around the church to the burial ground, where a newly dug grave was awaiting its guest.

"Heaven's morning breaks and earth's vain shadows flee.
In life, in death, O Lord ....."

Again the singing and praise was something to hear and behold.

The casket was gently lowered to the boards placed across the mouth of the resting place and straps were inserted to facilitate the final descent.

The minister had placed himself on top of the mound of newly dug soil so that he could look down upon the gathering, who were now tightly circled around, straining to peep down into the trench.

"Let us pray!"

Silence fell all around and it seemed as though the creatures of the woods ceased their twittering and foraging to respect the dead. Into the silence came a faint scratching sound, hardly discernible and difficult to ascertain from whence it came. Our preacher strained his ears to locate the source and location, many of the congregation looking at each other with questioning eyes, but nothing was determined.

"Let us pray" repeated the minister.

Rap-tap-tap.

The location of the sound was now clear! Something was knocking on the coffin lid.

A gasp arose from the mourners and the circle made a sudden increase in size as everyone took a backward step from the hole, some showing clear signs of agitation. Others clung to each other. Some called to heaven for guidance. A few turned away and made a rapid retreat from the scene, milling about at a fair distance away, disturbed and fearful.

"Good Lord preserve us."

Reverend Johnston had stepped down from the mound, but gathering his courage and faith in his Maker, he climbed back to his advantage point.

"Brethren! Sisters! We have come to mourn and bury our beloved brother, so let us be about our business."

He beckoned the pall bearers, who hesitated a moment, but witnessing the composure of their preacher, they stepped forward, lifted the coffin gently, held firm onto the hoisting straps, removed the planks and started the coffin on its final journey. The casket was halfway down the hole when all hell broke loose.

A terrific din burst from the coffin, the lid being subjected to heavy blows from within, the sound reverberating all around the bye-standers.

Panic ensued. The pall bearers let go of the straps as though they were red hot, so that the coffin plummeted downwards, to arrive with a sickening crash at its destination.

The congregation went absolutely berserk. Screaming, shouting, wailing, they took to their heels and fled, some seeking the sanctuary of the church, where they fell to their knees to pray, others racing, some up and some down the lane, heading for home where they imagined they would be safe.

As the commotion faded away, the woods fell strangely still again as if watching and waiting with bated breath for some unthinkable creature to spring from the grave.

Reverend Johnston was alone.

He stood unmoved, his paling knuckles clenched to his Bible, his eyes closed in prayer. With a deep sigh he opened his eyes, took measure of the scene before him and now that his flock had fled, he knew that he would have to fight the good fight all alone. He gazed to heaven for a fleeting moment, then shrugged his shoulders and tentatively approaching the grave, he looked down and spoke out with a quiet, gentle voice:

[1] "Nathaniel man! Yu fambly an frends wuk aad fi gi yu dis ya

---

[1] "Nathaniel man! Your family and friends have worked hard to give you this send off. They've given enough time to cook food to give the people. You've had a good service, so you might as well be satisfied with everything."

Dead, But He Won't Lie Down

sen aaf. Dey gi enuf time fi cuk food and gi di smady dem. Yu git a gud sarbis, so yu mite well satisfy wid ebry ting."

Then with a sudden surge of fervour and a pointing of his finger:

[2] "An di dacta se yu ded .....

..... so yu DED!"

---

[2] "And the doctor says you're dead ..... so you're dead!"

Do Puppies Have Duppies?

Do Puppies Have Duppies?

A man was riding a horse one dark night.
Near the cemetery he saw a puppy.

It looked up at him with its big brown eyes.

Climbing down, he put it in his coat.
The horse was jittery all the way home.

At his yard he climbed down, tethered the horse
And put the puppy down.

It looked up at him with its big brown eyes.

The man stepped up to his porch.
The puppy was back in his coat.

Puppy put down, puppy back, down and up
again.
No way could he put the puppy away.

Three weeks later the man was DEAD.

****

Four weeks later, a man was riding a horse.
Near the cemetery he saw a puppy .....!!!

The Legend of the Golden Table

This tale is associated with a very old Jamaican legend, reaching far back in time, when the sweet Arawak tribes farmed the fertile land of the island that they called Xaymaca, which in their original Arawak language meant 'the land of wood and water'.

These were happier times, before the Spanish Conquistadors arrived.

The Arawak people were the first recorded settlers, who made a remarkable journey in dug-out canoes from South America some time in the seventh century, bringing with them the cassava root, which is used to this day to make the flour for 'bammy' bread. They were a gentle, hospitable and peaceful community, but found themselves disturbed by a warlike tribe of cannibals from other parts of the Caribbean called the Caribs, so had to take up arms. Although many a battle took place between these two factions, the Arawaks maintained their friendly ways, to the surprise of Columbus when he arrived at Discovery Bay in 1494.

Christopher Columbus renamed the island Jamaica and called the inhabitants Indians, which he may have derived from the Spanish 'in Dios' or ' in God' or 'people of God,' referring to their peacefulness. This comment on their lifestyle, however, did not protect them from the slaughter and slavery that followed. Not only were they carried off to Spain in large numbers, they had no resistance to and were decimated by smallpox and other diseases brought by the invaders.

It would be difficult to make a date for this legend, but it would certainly have been at a time before the Arawaks discovered the treacherous nature of their conquerors. Again the location for this story is not clear, but as it took place in a steep rock-faced valley with a turbulent river at its base, a little exploration around the island might reveal an archaeological find or two. The Rio Cobre River Valley could make a good starting point.

The Arawaks in Jamaica have been totally exterminated as they did not last long after Spanish colonisation. It was a tragedy, especially as the invaders, finding no precious metals, soon lost interest in this beautiful island and little remains of their influence. The issue of gold is interesting, because the following legend is about a solid gold table owned by a local tribe of Indians. How did they possess such a treasure? Did they bring it with them from South America? As is the nature of folk lore, we may never know!

* * * * * * *

Chief Xoquetza stood in full ceremonial dress awaiting the arrival of his guests.

He wore the fan shaped headdress that marked his rank. He was naked, apart from a feathered skirt and a fine long feathered cloak, fastened at the neck. In his hand he held a beautifully carved wooden staff of office and he made a fine sight, his brown skin shining in the bright sunlight. When they were told of the approaching newcomers, the people of this Arawak village had all turned out to satisfy their curiosity. Nearly naked men, women and children milled around in ever increasing excitement as the time approached to entertain the guests from across the sea. They were a naive people, trusting and hospitable, so they had spent the day preparing a feast, laying it out on a large table made of solid gold, which stood in the centre of the village clearing.

Six visitors emerged from the bush.

It was some two years since Columbus had set foot on Xaymaca soil and the Spanish were about their business of occupation and rape. All such activity was usually preceded by smiling faces and forked tongues, so such a greeting was offered as they entered the clearing. The group consisted of soldiers, carrying muskets and pikes sloped across their shoulders, not intending to attack because they had been informed that this particular tribe was likely to be peaceful. Indeed they were, for as the Chief raised his hand in greeting the men of the tribe gathered around, touching the strange garments and weaponry, whilst the women showed a special interest in the facial hair of the newcomers. Communicating in signs and gestures, both sides sought to satisfy their curiosity, but the Spaniards certainly knew what was being conveyed when the Chief pointed to his mouth, then to the food laden table.

The feast began, but it didn't take long for Xoquetza to realise that his guests seemed to be more interested in the table than the food. He noticed that they were making silent signals to one another, as they pointed to and stroked the golden metal. He was not aware of its value, it being for him only a metal object of great beauty, but it was obvious that the soldiers coveted this tribal heirloom. He kept his counsel and still treated the visitors with courtesy until the Conquistadors returned to their encampment.

The moment they were gone, the Chief, to the amazement of his followers, had the golden table cleared, then removed to a place of hiding. This wily old fox had seen the greedy glint in the eyes of his guests and had anticipated their future actions.

His prophesy was soon to be fulfilled, for only two days later a small army, led by his previous visitors, entered and massacred his village, slaughtering without mercy the men, women and innocent children.

In the midst of this brutal havoc, Xoquetza was lashed to a tree to be witness to the genocide. Some of the children who were not butchered outright were strung up by their wrists to overhanging tree branches facing their chief.

Search as they may there was no sign of the golden table, so the silver tongued devil, who had first offered his Judas friendship to the Chief, now began a slow torture of his honourable host. He was skilled at his craft and inflicted appalling pain as he endeavoured to ascertain the whereabouts of the coveted prize, but the more torment he administered, the more stubborn his victim became, but this torturer had a sudden inspiration and giving a command to his men, turned attention to the hanging children. Dry wood and bracken was piled up under each one, then the first was set alight until the child was twisting and screaming in agony. This was too much for Xoquetza to bear, and he roared out in anguish for the child.

The evil Spaniard knew that he had found the mark, so he cut the grieving Chief down from the tree, shrugged his shoulders and pointed, to question the direction of travel to find the table. Xoquetza waved to be followed and staggered into the undergrowth, but no sooner had he left than the treacherous soldiers lit all of the fires, then followed behind, leaving the hanging children to burn to death.

They all wound their way towards the river, a fast running cataract that rushed down between high cliffs, the party picking a careful way upwards along a precarious trail, until it came upon a cave, high up in the steep rock face. The victim and his oppressor stepped into the dim light of the cavern and as their eyes adjusted to the darkness, the golden prize stood before them. The Spaniard gesticulated to instruct his prisoner to bring the table to the cave mouth and with one mighty heave the heavy ceremonial furniture was hoisted to chest height. Turning to find his captor between himself and the exit, Xoquetza let out a bellow of triumph as he charged, sweeping the tyrant before him. They both careered out onto the ledge and the table, Arawak and soldier tumbled over and over, down into the raging torrent below. Whilst the trophy sank into the depths, the two men were swept away to a watery grave.

* * * * * *

The following day a small group of soldiers returned equipped with rope and grappling hooks to dredge the river bottom for the precious artefact, but before they could commence their labour, the table floated to the surface. This hefty treasure rose up from the depths as though it were made of cork and sat quite still on the turbulent waters, glistening in the sunlight. For a moment the Spaniards stood awe struck at this extraordinary spectacle, but the value of the booty soon brought them back to earth. Grappling irons were cast time after time, until one lucky angler 'struck gold' and with a great 'whoop' of triumph, they all took a firm hold of his line and began to heave........but the table wouldn't budge. They strained to greater effort, when suddenly a guffaw of loud laughter rang from cliff to cliff. Turning towards the interruption, the figure of a native man was seen standing at the mouth of the cave, wearing a fan shaped headdress, a feathered skirt and a long feathered cloak and as he stood arms outstretched, he carried a wooden staff in his left hand.

My God! It was the duppy of Xoquetza, returned to protect the table of gold.

The men were transfixed with terror, when without warning, the Golden Table sank back into the river, dragging the screaming soldiers into the wild violent waters, never to be seen alive again.

* * * * * * *

During the past five hundred years since this incident, many brave souls have set out in search of the Arawak's gold, never to return. It is said that every day at noon, the table will rise to the surface of the rushing waters, sparkle in the sunlight, then sink once again, out of the reach of covetous hands.

If it is your intention to seek this illusive treasure, be prepared for an encounter with Xoquetza, whose laughter can often be heard ringing across the valley to this very day.

Home Sweet Home

This was the first time I heard of Jamaican duppies, it being the first story that Leonie told me, not long after we were married. I think it's a classic.

****

Francis rocked to and fro on the old chair that granddad had made for gandma. Sitting out on the veranda, life was great. It had been a hot sticky day and working in his smallholding was no easy task. Pigs and chickens to feed, hoeing, picking, lopping, the toil was never ending, but now he was finished for the day.

He had promised aunt Winnie earlier that week that he would visit and take her some ackee and other produce that might be appreciated, but he thought he would spoil himself by just rocking for a while. A few puffs on his chalk pipe did no harm either.

Basic as it was, Francis loved his home. He had a roof over his head to keep out the rain, a bed at night and food was always close by. A few steps from the house with machete in hand and there was sustenance aplenty just waiting to be harvested.

His wife Carmen was about her business beside the main road in Porus, where she sold oranges and grapefruits or whatever their few acres would provide. Life was hard for the two of them, but they always thanked God for all that he gave.

The children were well grown and prospering in England .... bless 'em!

[1] "O.K. Winnie! Me a cum," muttered Francis in reply to the voice of conscience sounding in his head.

With one last push, he rocked to his feet, jumped down the

---

[1] "O.K. Winnie, I'm coming."

veranda steps, picked up the basket of goodies left by the side of the house and strolled over to his donkey cart. There was considerable delay as Ben, the donkey, was not too keen to move from his grazing and only when it realised that Francis would have no nonsense did it submit to being hitched up and settle down to the task of pulling the cart.

They set off up the track past Arthur's workshop, where he chipped, sawed and chiselled each day to create fancy carved bed heads and the most excellent sturdy tables and chairs. Further on still they passed a church, then another and another. So many churches, all competing to have the longest names, some crudely painted on roughly hewn signs by the roadside.

The Church of God of Revelation
The Flame of Revival Pentecostal Church
The Open Bible Church of the Nazarene.

Francis and Carmen worshipped at the Baptist church, with its short name and short service.

Some friends and neighbours were out on their porches, taking advantage of a cooling breeze that had sprung up following an evening downpour of rain. A few exchanged greetings with Francis.

"What's up?"
"Weh yu a go man?"
"W'appen?"

The hill was steepening and Ben was needing constant goading to keep his mind on the job at hand. It was getting dark swiftly, as it seems to do in Jamaica. The dwellings were left behind and the world was becoming still and quiet and Francis was alone. He talked to Ben all of the time, but Ben was either not listening or was not interested, because he never replied.

[2] "Good, me wi get comp'ny now."

Just ahead a solitary dark figure was walking languorously up

---

[2] "Good, I'll get some company now."

the track. Francis drew alongside, but the stranger walked on without paying any heed, wearily dragging his bare feet. He did look a pitiful sight.

[3] "Cum yah Man! Mi wi tek yu home."

The young man stopped, turning to face the cart.

[4] "Oh! What a dutty bwoy."

He was unkempt, as though he hadn't washed or tidied himself for days. His dreadlocks were all matted together, hanging down over his protruding eyes in straggly lumps. White streaks ran down the black face, making his skin seem almost fluorescent in the darkness. His T-shirt, full of holes, had shrunk to his ribs and his trousers were torn to ribbons.

Francis regretted having stopped.

[5] "Weh yu cum fram bwoy?"

The man just pointed down the road with his long bony fingers.

[6] "Hap up pan de caat."

Francis extended a hand to help the boy, who grasped hold with a tight bony grip and jumped up alongside the driver.

[7] "Bwoy what a waay yu an cole."

Ben faltered a step, then trotted along with ease as the cart topped the crest of the hill and started down the other side.

Francis liked a good conversation so he started to chat away, as he often did with the boys in the bar.

The stranger sat silent. He seemed to be listening, making what could be described as a grunt here and there, but he never offered any verbal response. Francis didn't mind. He just droned on and on.

It was no surprise that he talked mostly about his [8]yard, about Carmen, about the kids, about aunt Winnie, about cousins and uncles, parents and grandparents, about Ben and grandma's rocking chair. He talked about friends and neighbours and the state of the local community, but always he came back to home sweet

---

[3] "Come here man. I'll take you home." [8] "Home."
[4] "Oh! What a dirty boy."
[5] "Where do you come from boy?"
[6] "Climb up on the cart."
[7] "Boy, your fingers are cold."

home. Eventually he ran out of steam, falling into meditative silence, with just the occasional flick of the reins and click of his teeth for Ben's benefit.

[9] "Tank yu sir. Me ketch a mi yard now."

Francis drew in the reins.

The passenger slid from the cart, sauntered around the back, crossed the road and walked through the gates of the cemetery. I say *through* the gates because they were closed and fastened tightly with iron chains at the time. Francis's eyes popped from his head and he let out a loud scream of terror. Ben reared up on his hind legs in fright, then galloped off down the road as if all the demons from hell were after him.

Aunt Winnie never had ackee that night.

Francis took the long way back to his yard and it was many a month that elapsed before he would venture past the cemetery gates during the day

..... he never did at night!!

---

[9] "Thank you sir. I've arrived home now."

Home Sweet Home

An English Duppy Story

This is a story illustrating that wherever Jamaican folks live, anywhere in the world, duppies are bound to follow. An amusing tale, it was brought to light by Pearl, a good friend of both Leonie and me.

****

Poor Albert!

Every day was a drudgery.

Ethel had died five months ago. Her blood pressure had caught up with her and she had passed over after suffering from a stroke.

Ethel had a grand funeral. Family and friends had come from far and near to pay their respects during the wake. Food was never ending, drinks flowed, hugs and kisses were exchanged and duppy stories were told, just like in the old days.

Now Albert was alone.

His allotment was showing signs of neglect and his visits to Ethel's graveside were becoming less and less frequent. There were signs that his mourning was turning into depression. Two weeks had passed since he last talked to Ethel, asking her why she had left him so alone but she never had a word to say.

This January day was crisp and cold and Albert didn't seem to have the energy to make an effort to do anything. As he dozed in front of the fire, he started to reminisce about hot sunny days back home in Jamaica. The warmth of his thoughts brightened him up for a few brief moments, but soon the familiar gloom of loneliness welled back over him.

"Dis won't do." Albert shook himself and resolved to go out for a walk.

[1] "Mek mi git up an' go visit Etel!"

He had not shaved and his shoes could have done with a good clean.

[2] "Mi no caa ow mi tan."

He put on coat, hat and scarf and made his way to the cemetery. Up the centre aisle, second left and third grave from the end.

IN LOVING MEMORY OF MY DEAR WIFE ETHEL

The dead flowers on the grave stone gave an air of neglect, so Albert removed them and placed them in the litter bin, hoping that if he tidied up a little he might feel less guilty.

[3] "Lawd Etel! Mi lonely yu si. Mi miss yu bad man."

[4] "Mi naa believe yu man. Weh yu de fi two weeks now? Luk pan 'ow yu tan. Yu shoes dutty and yu no shave."

For a moment Albert was transfixed to the spot and his jaw dropped in amazement.

[5] "Who dat?"

He took to his heels and ran almost to the gates, shaking from head to foot, breathing like an old steam engine, where he stood in panic for some minutes. It took some pluck, I tell you, for him to tiptoe cautiously back to the grave.

[6] "Etel, a yu dat?" he whispered.

[7] "Who you tink den?" came the reply from below the tomb stone.

[8] "Lawd, Gawd, yu a duppy?"

---

[1] "I must get up and go to visit Ethel!"
[2] "I don't care how I look."
[3] "Lord Ethel, I'm lonely. I miss you."
[4] "I don't believe you man. Where have you been for the last two weeks?
     Look at the state you're in. Your shoes are dirty and you haven't shaved."
[5] "Who's that?"
[6] "Ethel, is that you?"
[7] "Who else would I be?"
[8] "Lord God! Are you a ghost?"

An English Duppy Story

[9] "So!"

Albert was gathering himself together.

[10] "Wah yu waan fram mi now?"

[11] "Mek mi tell yu. Dem adda one dem a ded fi some rice an' peas. Gwan go get some bring cum."

Albert's courage was returning and the banter with Ethel's duppy was cheering him up no end.

[12] "Weh mek ye cyaan go yu self?"

After a brief pause Ethel said with an air of impatience:

[13] "We cyaan go, caas wi no hab no draws on."

Albert stood gob-struck and then as he realised how ludicrous this remark was, he sniggered. Then he laughed and he laughed until his sides were about to split.

Albert died the following year and was laid to rest with his dear Ethel.

It is said that if you should walk by the cemetery at night you can hear talking and laughter well into the early hours of the morning. Some say it's Albert and Ethel.

I wonder if Ethel and her duppy friends ever did get their rice and peas?

---

[9] "What else would I be?"

[10] "What do you want from me now?"

[11] "Let me tell you. The others are dying for some rice and peas. Go and get some for us."

[12] "Why can't you go yourself?"

[13] "We can't go, because we have no knickers on."

Obeah Versus Obeah

Obeah is African in origin, being introduced into Jamaica during the black days of slavery. I believe that in the Ashanti language *Obay'Fo* means wizard and *Obi* in East Africa means sorcery.

Obeah practice in the West Indies could also have been influenced by European Christian colonisers, who themselves believed in witchcraft because a belief in ghosts was strong in Scotland and England, where many of the plantation owners of Jamaica originated.

English witches collected hair combings and sweat soaked clothes to use them against their intended victims, which is apparently also an Obeah practice. White and black superstitions are clearly merged.

So what is Obeah?

It is the belief that spirits may be employed to harm the living or be called off from such mischief. Spells and amulets are required to keep duppies under control. Obeah practitioners, like their African medicine men counterparts are also skilled in the use of herbal medicines and poisons.

Excellent information about recorded cases of Obeah practitioners being brought to court, can be found at the National Library of Jamaica in Kingston, which is a first class source of folklore history.

* * * * * * *

My wife Leonie sat in our living room enjoying the chat that goes along with having her hair done. Her hairdresser told us this ugly story that she had heard from her father.

****

There was this man who had two women, the one his wife, the other his mistress. His wife was pregnant and like many dutiful wives, wanted a dutiful husband to stay close by her, but he spent most of his time with his 'sweetheart'. Seven nights a week he stayed out and he only came home for his laundry or when he felt hungry.

His wife wanted him to herself, so she paid a visit to a local Obeah woman, who listened patiently as the misused wife unburdened herself. She pleaded and pleaded to the Obeah woman for a spell to bring back the wandering partner to his yard.

"No problem," and the Obeah woman explained what was to be done.

A pan of soup was to be prepared ready for one of his hunger visits and to this tantalising dish was to be added his wife's body fluids ..... Yes! her body fluids. Well, can you imagine?

This, however, she duly did, presenting it to her man, who ate it up with great relish. Nothing happened, but on a return visit to the 'alternative medicine' doctor, she was counselled to be patient and lo and behold, during the following week things started to move.

Her husband came home on the thursday night and he even gave her a little. The following week he stayed home twice and week by week, little by little, he was at home more and more until, praise be, he was stopping home all the time and seemed happy to do so.

Some while later the mistress came banging on his door to see w'appen, but the good wife gave her a good cussing and told her not to come back in her yard ..... [1]'warra, warra, warra!'

Revenge was now the issue. The 'sweetheart' went straight way to an Obeah man of some reputation, to tell her story of woe,

---

[1] Respectable cussing. She would have said far worse really.

but we are already familiar with his advice. Yes! to make a stew, putting in "your bodily juices and get your victim to eat." Taking the pot to her wayward lover (the wife was out) she offered it as a farewell gift.

When the wife came home she was, of course, curious to know from whence came the pot of stew, so her husband lied that he had cooked for her. After her first shock of disbelief, she assumed that this was an extra bonus from the Obeah woman's magic, so she dished out the hot soup and they both set to with a will and it was good.

The wife felt 'strange' for a few days but the effect soon passed. Not so for the husband, for his condition took a backward turn. He took to laying in his bed until late in the morning and then he stopped going to work altogether.

"Mi no 'appy." she said to the Obeah woman as she related how well life had improved with the spell at first, but how things had now gone from one extreme to another.

"Dis should no 'appen" was the reply, so after a lengthy cogitation she asked for some time to investigate how to solve the dilemma and would the wife kindly come back in a few days.

The wife went home most upset, taking it out on her husband, cussing and nagging until he confessed about the soup and the visit by his mistress. Oh! what a row that followed, the wife easily winning on points, almost a knockout. She then ran to the yard of her husband's lover for another confrontation, but was only met by a hands-on-hip sneer.

[2] "Mi nu waan im now. Im naa wuk, so im nu ab nu moni."

Turning away the wife set off straight way to the Obeah woman to tell of the conflict and how she now suspected that a counter spell had been administered to her husband..... but she already knew.

****

Now we must leave this man, his wife and his mistress to their own destinies, as our tale moves on to its ugly climax.

---

[2] "I don't want him now. He's not working so he has no money."

****

Our Obeah woman was really vexed now, not at all pleased that some other practitioner was interfering with her business. She spent all that morning muttering to herself, letting fly with the occasional curse as she painstakingly mixed up a nasty looking concoction.

The day before she had sent out her spies and was able to locate and identify her competitor, so with brew in hand she made her way to his front door to knock loudly three times, turning on the spot between each blow, a ritual that was to intensify her magic.

As the Obeah man stepped from his house, he was greeted by a shrill cry as she flung the fluid full into his face, then she ran back to her yard, screaming, gyrating and cussin' all the way. Staggering back in surprise, the Obeah man clutched his face as the corrosive lotion started to burn and strip the skin from his cheeks. He rushed to the room where he kept his own supply of powders, herbs and suchlike and started to nurse his face with special medicinals. To no avail.

Not many people knew that he was an Obeah man, or should I rather say that most folks knew, but would not own up to it, because this profession instilled fear in the local community. Business was kept 'private,' so he couldn't turn to anyone for help. He wasn't, however, going to be able to keep this incident private for long, because his face was exfoliating most horribly. He applied aloe vera lotion, cocoa-butter lotion and a number of special magical unctions that are only known to Obeah practitioners, but nothing gave relief, so he was reduced to the ancient recipe of making a paste from the dirt of his yard, which he plastered as a pack liberally over his face. But still to no avail.

A visit to the local doctor was just as futile, as the prescribed medication had no effect whatsoever. By this time, any skin that was not peeling, was developing large yellow blisters that itched and itched and itched.

The final straw came late that night, as he was scratching and begging for the curse to be lifted. The pus filled blisters began to burst and to his horror, the fluid seemed to 'wriggle' down his cheeks. His face was covered in maggots, horrible, squirming, wriggling, maggots.

Emitting a piercing cry of pain and terror, he fled from the house, vomiting with revulsion and calling for help, but when the local householders cast eyes upon this macabre spectacle, they ran indoors, barricading the doors fast. This ghastly sight blundered from yard to yard, knocking on door after door, as the maggots emerged from his nose, ears and mouth. Our Obeah man eventually ran off into the bush, his cries being heard throughout the night, as he staggered and stumbled through the undergrowth.

****

A week later his decaying maggoty corpse was found lying in a gully.

Nobody wanted to claim it. Nobody wanted to bury it. The church would not consider the body being placed in consecrated ground, but the stench from his house where it had been placed became so nauseating that some arrangement just had to be made.

A sepulchre was built in a remote place on top of Coffee Grove Hill and the few spectators who dared to accompany the coffin, hastily slid the box into the ground and it was promptly mortared up. There was no Minister to say a prayer over the remains, no hymns were sung. Just a hasty retreat from the scene.

They were but thirty paces from the tomb when a resounding crash reverberated across the valley. Running back they saw that the concrete roof of the Obeah man's resting place had shattered and collapsed onto the coffin lid, breaking it wide open. Amongst the broken stone and timber, the rotting corpse was clearly seen, maggots crawling from every orifice ..... but it was moving ..... it was 'alive'!

The small group cringed back as a hollow voice came from the tomb:

"Leave me aloone. Leave me aloone."

60

Obeah versus Obeah

****

Nobody ever visits this part of the hill anymore, but it is rumoured that if you are ever passing too closely by, at certain times of the year you will hear our Obeah man cry:

"Leave me aloone."

"Leave me aloone."

The Boy and the Barble Dove

This pretty story was told to me by a roadside roast yam seller, on Melrose Hill on the old road from Mandeville to Porus.

****

A young boy went out hunting one day.
He shot a bird dead and carried it home.

The Barble Dove began to sing:
"Tek aff mi fedder. Tek aff mi fedder."
So the boy plucked the bird.

The Barble Dove sang:
"Cut mi up. Cut mi up."
So the boy chopped the bird into portions.

The Barble Dove sang:
"Spice mi up. Spice mi up."
So the boy rubbed it with black pepper, onions and curry.

The Barble Dove sang:
"Cuk mi up. Cuk mi up."
So the boy fried the portions in a Dutch pot.

Barble Dove

The Barble Dove sang:
[1] "Memba fi yu Granni. Memba fi yu Granni."
But the greedy boy ate it all up himself.

The boy became ill, took to his bed and his belly swell.
His belly burst and im DED.

The Barble Dove's Duppy came out of his belly
and flew away singing:

"Im who shot dis bird, 'im DED!!"

---

[1] "Remember to give your Grandma some."

The Sweet Toothed Duppy

If you are ever travelling along the coastal road somewhere near Lucea in the Parish of Hanover, you may come across a small folk museum. This delightful facility that is the Hanover Historical Society, will introduce you to a microcosm of Jamaican rural activities that are now passing away, as our modern times encroach upon the simple life. Here you will find water cooling pots, the refrigeration units of the time and spiked orange rinders. A cassava press and sieve made from basket weave and pottery platters to cook the bammy on open wood fires. A small plot of traditional crops, like cotton, pineapple, sweet potato, tobacco, corn and sugar cane of course. There is an example of a home made sugar cane crusher, a simple device for squeezing out the juice from the many jointed stems. The fluid was then boiled until it made a syrup which was called 'wet sugar.' Further boiling creates a thicker product, which when left to cool in a can, becomes hard 'head sugar.' During this process the householders would sometimes add ginger, to be eaten later with coconut. With the advent of modern sugar refineries this activity is now dead, so that you are unlikely to see the farmers carrying wet and head sugar to market. This traditional tale takes place when there was still a little money to be made from hand crushing your own cane.

* * * * * * *

Frederick farmed his few acres close by Kent village in the Parish of St. Catherine. This particular morning, he had loaded up the donkey cart with yam, oranges, ackee and other produce to sell at Spanish Town market, just six miles down the road that skirts the Rio Cobra river. He was also carrying a considerable amount of wet and head sugar, that he had recently crushed and boiled, following a good harvest of cane.

All was going well as he walked beside the jackass, bridle in hand. It was still before the dawning of the sun and the roadside vegetation was shrouded in dew, that hung like pearls on the industrious spider's webs, covering everything with miraculously complex patterns. Nothing stirred to disturb Fred's reverie, as he shuffled down the track towards the town once called St Jago de la Vega, founded in 1538 during the Spanish occupation of the island. So preoccupied was he with his thoughts, Fred failed to notice that some leakage in one of his barrels was allowing a thin trail of wet sugar to form on the road behind them.

Now a mischief of duppies was skulking about in the bush not many paces from the track and the sweet smell of the absconding fluid drifted to the nostrils of one of these roguish spirits. It stopped in its tracks, for a moment went all stiff and then began to shiver and shake with rapture. Nothing pleases a duppy more than the taste of sugar, so it started to sniff the air to track down the alluring nectar. As though in a trance, our intoxicated duppy took one step here, then two steps there, raising its head to lock onto the candy fragrance. Slowly it was pulled to the road and the trickle of delight that was spilling from the cart. The other duppies watched as their companion rushed forward, threw itself down on all fours and began to lap up the enticing juice. Lick! lick! Slurp! slurp!

Soon the ghost raised its head to say:

[1] "Den if a di sulalup so sweet, how tan di head?"

Frederick heard this remark and turned to investigate this intrusion into his preoccupation. Taking up a stick, he rushed back to thwack the thief about the head, until it beat a hasty retreat back into the bush. Not for long however, for no sooner

---

[1] "Then if the syrup is so sweet, the head sugar is sweeter?"

did our farmer return to his donkey to continue the journey, than the scoundrel sneaked back to his sugary delight.

The cart was approaching the Flat Bridge, a notorious river crossing that was highly dangerous during the rainy season. Turning sharply at right angles to the road, the simple structure traverses the waters, supported by two pontoon shaped pillars that lead intrepid travellers to another sharp bend back onto the road towards Spanish Town. No hazard presented itself on this particular occasion, because the river was not impatient to be on its way, but there were times in October or May when the heavy rains fell, that it would be foolish to navigate the crossing.

The swollen and turbulent waters would rise so high, that the road itself would be awash with wild rushing currents, all quite capable of sweeping our farmer, cart and donkey away down river to the sea. Many a life had been lost, when senseless travellers challenged the merciless Rio Cobre.

Frederick and his donkey cart were nearly half way over when the sugar robber made a bold move. Rushing forward, it leapt up onto the cart to search for the cans of 'head,' but before it succeeded in its mission, the farmer angrily turned to defend the hard earned fruits of his labour.

This duppy was in for a fearsome shock. Being licked with a stick was no deterrent for a sweet toothed ghost, but it was now about to be flogged with a 'cow cod' whip. This implement was made from the spinal cord of a cow and if held and used in the left hand, it causes great consternation amongst the duppy fraternity. They don't like it laid on 'em, they really don't, so cracking his cow cod in the air and running to the back of the cart to cut off the duppies retreat, Fred slashed the bewildered spirit hard across its back.

One, two, three stinging blows rained down on our howling duppy, who screamed for mercy and before the farmer could deliver number four, the spook leapt out of range of this painful encounter. Off the cart it dived, clearing the bridge, to tumble down to the river below, where it stood dejected and fearful, up to its waist in the murky waters.

The duppy's companions had been fearful observers of the

plight of their friend and now ran to the bank to be of assistance, crying out to the farmer to leave their pal alone. They called out to their downcast mate:

² "Johnoy! Wah a brute of a lick dis!"

³ "Ano so much de brute of a lick" replied Johnoy, "but a frighten mi frighten!"

---

² "Johnoy! What a mighty blow!"
³ "It wasn't so much the blow, but I was so very frightened!"

The Man Who Stayed Out Late

This is an experience of my wife's Pappa.

****

Alex was prone to staying out late at night and those were the days when there was no electricity, thus no street lighting, so that the only light to see you home was from the moon.

This eventful evening our man was playing dominoes with his cronies at Maas Arthur's shop, so between them a few white rums would never return to the bottle.

As usual, it was getting late as conversation turned to things that go bump in the night. Joking and laughing, the boys suggested that Alex sleep over, for it was a dark night and the duppies would be out and about.

Taking no heed of such nonsense he set out for home, walking the familiar route across the road to the Police Station, then off up the lane towards the railway. Even in the dark Alex knew this journey well. Just ahead of him he saw someone walking his way. The dark shape of a man in black who disappeared into the Railway Station at the Porus Crossing.

When the railway was running, station workers wore black suits. They had sleeping quarters just up the lane on the right so that they could bed down for the night, to be ready for an early start to run the engine and coaches back to Kingston. A service

The Man Who Stayed Out Late

from Kingston to Montego Bay was running in those days – it stopped around 1982. Alex assumed that the figure was a railway man, so didn't take much notice and he walked on.

When he was getting close to Mother Bryant's Hill, where the shop that Kay used to own still stands (there was nothing but bush in those days), his head 'raised.' This was an old expression which described the sensation in the head that accompanies fear.

Taking off his hat, he quickly turned it inside out, which was one of many rituals that might ward off a duppy.

Then he saw it – a most awesome sight. A giant man was standing astride the road ahead, one great boot on the railway line, whilst the other was near the house of Miss Miranda the hairdresser, a good forty paces between each foot.

This vast figure rose high into the sky, looking down on Alex with red flaming eyes that dripped fire.

The appalling apparition began to reach out for pappa, but quick as a shot Alex put his cap under his arm and ran for dear life, straight under the duppy's legs. He ran like fire for home, rushing through the door into the arms of his mother. He was speechless and unable to tell his story until the following day.

Two mornings later pappa was visited by a man from the village, who described a dream he had at the same time as Alex's encounter with the duppy, in which he described in detail the events of that scary night and he warned father not to do it again – stay out late that is – or pappa would be sorry!

This threat, we know, never did stop pappa and he could not be persuaded from staying out late at night

– doing who knows what!!!

The Duppies of Rose Hall

Have you ever paid a visit to the notorious house they call Rose Hall?

If you find yourself in Montego Bay on the north coast of Jamaica in the parish of St James, you would be well advised to travel some eight or nine miles along the road by the sea that takes you through Little River, to find the white stone residence of the late Annie Palmer.

The building of the house began in the late eighteenth century by a Henry Fanning, on three hundred acres of good cane land, with a marvellous view of the sea to the north. Six months into the project poor Henry died. Some years later, his rich widow Rosa married a planter by the name of George Ash, who finished the work on the Mediterranean styled big house. After its completion George also passed away. Strange how many of the masters of the house were destined to have a short life span in this cursed building! A pity really, because the Hall itself is delightful, with its double flight of stone steps that lead up to an open terrace, taking us to the main entrance of this impressive double storey dwelling place. Inside we discover a superb mahogany staircase that leads from the hall up to the infamous bedrooms, where many men were to meet their Maker.

The notoriety of Rose Hall began on March the twenty-eighth in the year of our Lord eighteen twenty, as John Rose Palmer, the nephew of the first John Palmer (who was the fourth husband of Rosa), entered his new home with his seventeen year old bride, Anne Mary Paterson, an outstandingly beautiful and proud young woman of Irish descent.

This union was doomed to failure.

John was cold and undemonstrative, but Annie was sensual

and excitement seeking, so it was of no surprise that some time after the wedding her husband discovered that she was having a clandestine affair with a plantation slave.

John gave her a severe beating, so she poisoned him and he died an agonising death.

No-one discovered her crime of revenge, but the slave had, unfortunately for him, been a witness and collaborator, so this loose end had to be dealt with. Now we begin to see the dark personality emerge, that led to Annie eventually being called a White Witch.

She had her current black lover bound and gagged on some trumped up charge and as she sat on a black steed she watched with great pleasure, as he was savagely beaten to an excruciating death.

So her reign of terror began.

As a child, her Haitian nurse maid had taught her the craft of Voodoo, which she used to subdue any rebellion amongst the slaves, that might have been caused by her cruel task mistress ways. To this day we can visit the dungeon in the cellar where dissidents were imprisoned and punished with spiked iron collars and chains, augmented by stocks and the flogging post. Although such activity was not uncommon on sugar plantations as the supervisors maintained 'discipline' amongst the slave workers, Annie enjoyed sadistic satisfaction by watching these horrendous 'corrections'.

One moment she would be enjoying the sexual orgies that she held in the house with her ebony servants and the next day she would be having them flogged for no good reason.

Retribution, however, was looming ever closer, but Annie blindly pursued her constant quest to relieve her boredom and satiate her passion. During this 'busy' time, Annie was still able to court and marry three more husbands and in spite of controversy over their demise, the opinion persists that two of them likely came to a 'sticky' end at the hands of our restless witch, along with many of her secret lovers.

One incident that illustrated how appalling was the state of affairs on the plantation, began when some of the slaves took their troubles to the local Obeah man. He was, and still is, the

Jamaican equivalent of the Voodoo priest who had the power to summon up spirits or duppies to wreak mischief on chosen victims. On this occasion the Obeah man was asked to use his skill with poisons to bring Annee down. He recruited a house servant by the name of Princess, who administered the bane in a glass of milk. Her mistress, however, noticed something wrong, had the milk analysed and took her attackers to court on charges of attempted murder. Three defendants stood in the dock ; the Obeah man, the cook and Princess. In spite of the testimony by Mrs Palmer, the first two managed to be acquitted, but not so the unfortunate Princess, who was hanged and her head delivered to the white witch. This gory sight was then thrust onto a bamboo stake and displayed for all of the slaves to see. Annee had won her battle with the Obeah man and once more the black workers were in terror of her magic.

The prophetic 'As ye sow so shall ye reap' was soon to be fulfilled. Annee was in turn to die in macabre circumstances. Some say that she was strangled by a lover, others that she was raped, then beaten to death. Yet again was she hanged and burned, or was she maimed and left to die in deserved agony? Legend and fact become difficult to differentiate, but one thing we know for certain is that Annee did not die of natural causes and with her dying breath she cursed the Great House and the land on which it stood.

So she was buried in a stone tomb not far from the Hall, but she had promised that her 'life force' would always be close by. To validate this vow, in 1930 a famous medium testified that she felt the presence of a restless spirit not far from the house. In the year 1959, another clairvoyant promised to summon the White Witch from her grave, but he reneged on his assurance with excuses that the gathered crowd were too noisy and that the moon was not set right. This event was reported by the *Daily Gleaner* on the sixth day of October. There is no doubt that the duppy of the last mistress of Rose Hall continues to revisit the scene of her hideous atrocities, for in the master bedroom, there are occasions when you may see her reflection in the wall mirror.

For myself I can rely on the witness of a good friend, whose encounter with Annie's duppy is recorded in the following tale.

* * * * * * *

My name is Alex Phillips.

This story concerns the time that I came to Jamaica from England, to enjoy two weeks holiday in the sun. Staying in Montego Bay at a very pleasant budget hotel called the Blue Harbour, I had suspended a mosquito net from the ceiling of my bedroom to protect me from these unwelcome blood seekers. These wee gnats were the only down side to my frequent visits to the land of 'wood and water.' I'm sure that they queue up at the Donald Sangster Airport, awaiting for my arrival, drooling and impatient to suck my life juices and leave me with those horrible itching bumps on my white protesting skin.

On this occasion, however, I had learned from previous experiences to come well prepared with soothing lotions and had purchased my two week's supply of 'Off' repellent, so all was going well.

On the third day of my stay, I was enjoying a cool dip in the hotel pool, when I struck up conversation with another guest who was relaxing on the steps sipping a rum and Coke. He was a Jamaican man, proud of his heritage, full of useful information about his native land and he was able to advise me about interesting places to visit. He suggested that I might find the local attraction of the Great House of Rose Hall most fascinating, so when he hinted that the place was haunted I promptly made arrangements to have a day trip to meet this Annie Palmer, whom he had introduced with such fervour. I was susceptible to a good ghost story and as a child had been fascinated by my father who was a great spinner of yarns that were stranger than fiction.

The following day I set out to look in on the last mistress of the Great House.

The tour guide was fascinating as she outlined the history of this infamous dwelling place. The house had apparently been allowed to fall into decay after the mistress died, as no-one seemed too keen to stay and suffer the consequences of her dying curse. Little of the interior survived, but an American couple had purchased the house and lovingly restored it to its original colonial splendour, rejuvenating its history and legends and opening the home to the public. It really was a most splendid abode, but I was most taken up by the stories of dungeons, tortures, debauchery and murder most foul. We were taken to the bedrooms where Mrs. Palmer despatched three of her four husbands, one of whom was purported to have left a large bloodstain on a carpet, which stayed right up to the time of renovation. Images were there for all to witness of photographs taken by tourists of the spectral faces that reflect from mirrors and windows in the Master bedroom.

Spending a short intermission in the cool pub, which was originally the ghastly dungeon, we were taken outside to view the tomb of the unlamented white witch. I couldn't quite put my finger on it, but there was something eerie that seemed to exude from this simple sepulchre. Many of the party found it difficult to stand close to the tomb and soon left the grounds and returned to the more agreeable comfort of the bar.

For myself, however, I couldn't resist an urge to stand alone by the rough memorial, to have a private 'conversation' with our decomposed tenant. I was hooked and fascinated by the possibility that the occupant's ghost was still at home and as I stood, resting the palms of my hands on the curved roof of her vault, I seemed to be taken over by a force that caused me to shudder as though an icy wind had just passed by. I became determined to check out the validity of these reports of strange manifestations surrounding the Great House legend.

At night the premises would be locked and secure, so that the possibility of a night vigil in one of the macabre bedrooms would have been out of the question, but passing the witching hours near the grave might be a possibility. So I left the attraction, returned to my hotel to eat and refresh myself with a siesta to prepare for a duppy hunt that night.

Just before midnight, I was skulking in the vicinity of Rose Hall.

On the lookout for security guards, I stealthily crept through the grounds, making my way to the back of the house where the sepulchre was located, sitting all alone on its bed of sea stones. Here and there palm trees grew on the bauxite red soil, interspersed by small evergreen shrubs. It was a bright moonlight night and the shadows of the palm leaves swaying in the night breeze created an unearthly feeling of an unseen presence. I couldn't resist running my fingers over the mottled stone of Annie's resting place and once again was overwhelmed by a bone striking chill.

"I know you're there, Mrs Palmer. I've come to visit you!"

I couldn't believe my own audacity, but I did notice how dry my mouth was as I spoke those bold words of invitation. Pussyfooting my way between the trees, I found concealment some fifty paces from her grave and settled down to wait for her spirit to awaken. So the long night of surveillance began. The uneasy silence was only disturbed by the rustling of dry leaves blown about by the gentle night wind, making a soft accompaniment for the distant call of a night owl, who was patiently waiting to swoop down on some luckless nocturnal creature. I was unable to fight off the soporific effect of this night music and my head began to loll and my eyes began to close. I slept soundly.

Suddenly I was startled back to my duppy watch. Something had run across my outstretched legs, causing my heart to skip a beat as I hastily returned from my sinister dreams, but I whispered a sigh of relief as I caught sight of a mongoose scuttling away, intent on pursuing an early morning feast. My watch indicated that it was now half past one and I was starting to feel a coldness that didn't seem to match the balmy night. Something drew my attention towards the Great House. It was far off voices calling out from inside and as the sound drew closer, I was able to discern the cry of "Miss Palmer, Miss Palmer!" Then to my consternation the figure of a man emerged from the abode, passing directly out through the large stone blocks of the white wall. Then another and yet another, all heading towards the object of my vigil. As they came closer, I observed that these miserable souls were dragging iron collared chains around neck, wrists and ankles. They were marked by the terrible beatings suffered in life. As they approached Annie's grave, they were joined by a number of white duppies, all of whom screamed in agony as they clutched at their poisoned throats. A decapitated black woman entered the unfolding play, carrying in outstretched arms, a screeching head that cried : "Revenge! Revenge!"

Gathering around the tomb, they wailed for Annie to come forth and to my alarm, she did as they bid. Yes! There stood Mrs. Annie Mary Palmer, as arrogant in death as in her notorious life, wielding her riding crop and hurling curses on these poor victims of her murderous reign. Not for long, however, for these spectres were no longer in fear of this mistress of Voodoo and they hurled themselves upon the spitting and swearing author of their sorrows.

I watched in mounting fear, as the infamous criminal was subjected to her everlasting punishment. She was dragged and bound to a palm tree and there she was flogged over and over again until her bleeding skin hung in shreds from her back. She was then ripped down and the vengeful gathering burned her with flaming torches. I cringed with revulsion at this terrible vengeance being laid at the feet of the White Witch and in spite of her dire history, it became too much to bear to see her suffering and to know that this would be her punishment, night after night for all eternity.

Without realising what I was doing, I rose to my feet and called out for mercy. This was a foolish mistake, for I immediately drew attention to my unwelcome presence. I stood petrified to the spot as the vicious group turned and with red eyes blazing, clanked their way towards me.

Moments later my underwear needed a visit to the laundry, so I turned on my heels and I ran and I ran down to the main road and started off hot foot for Montego Bay.

Luckily for me I was picked up by a police patrol, who took me to my hotel, as I rambled on about red eyed duppies. The officer gave me a warning about too much rum, but left me with a friendly smile.

As I stripped off to enter the shower I glanced into the bathroom mirror......

......my hair had turned white!

House for Rent

A lady lived in a house that was located in the cemetery next to the church. It had been built there many years before to accommodate the priest, but he stayed in the residence only a few days, before moving to another house, further away from the church.

Next came three nuns, but their stay was just as short lived. Following some sort of 'fuss', they went their different ways.

After a meeting of the church council the decision was made to rent the house to 'suitable' members of the congregation. No-one stayed long and the house was subject to rumours and speculations, but as usual no-one could provide anything concrete.

Well, as I said, this lady was renting the house. One Sunday evening she was dressing in her best clothes, preparing to go to the church service, when she took over faint, feeling suddenly so unwell that she had to go to bed. No sooner did she climb between the sheets than she fell into a deep sleep.

It was dark now and she became restive and was easily disturbed by the sound of high heeled shoes click-click-clicking up the path and onto the porch.

Then came a hollow sounding beating on the front door.

Our lady lay very still and for no accountable reason began to shiver, as though the night air had suddenly become chill. The rapping resumed.

Something told her that it was a duppy, so she screamed a terrible scream.

[1] "Weh mi Bible, weh mi Bible?" she cried

Whoever or whatever was outside just laughed, a sardonic sort of laugh and replied:

[2] "Yu Bible nu gud, yu Bible nu gud. Me used to aal dat!"

The lady of the house crossed herself, dived under the sheets, covering her head, shaking with fright and remained so for ages until a sleep of exhaustion fell upon her. She slept on and on in a trance so deep, that the priest (having missed her at the service the previous evening) had to pound on the door until it broke and shake her robustly before she would arouse from her slumber. She broke into hysterical tears, spluttering and stuttering her story to the concerned priest and as they both started to share their fears they endeavoured to explain the frightful experience.

The hidden secret of this haunted house began to come out and all of the repressed superstitious fears surrounding tales of duppies were openly discussed by the priest.

He believed that, because the house had been built over old graves in the burying ground, some spirit or other had been disturbed so that it came back again and again to knock on the house door, expressing its displeasure at the intruding tenants.

Clearly things were so bad that no-one lived long in the house, always being driven to despair by our mischievous spirit.

Does anyone wish to rent a very desirable house in the Parish?

---

[1] "Where's my bible?"
[2] "Your Bible's no good. I'm used to all that."

Did You Know? (2)

That scorpions will be driven away if you spit and say: "Our Father, Our Father."

* * * * * * *

That Obeah men may throw graveyard dirt onto your zinc roof.

This will draw duppies to rattle around your yard every night until the soil is removed. You may also fall into a trance-like sleep and remain so until the wind blows the dirt away.

* * * * * * *

That if the Crocodile man visits he will knock three times. Whatever you do, do NOT answer!

(You will find this character in the final tale of this volume)

* * * * * * *

That if you meet a duppy you can protect yourself by turning your hat inside out.

* * * * * * *

That you may be doomed if you are bitten by a Galliwasp lizard.

If you are unfortunate enough to be so attacked, you must rush forthwith, to get to water before this reptile does so. If you do, the galliwasp will die and you will be safe. If he beats you to it, however, your fate is sealed.

* * * * * *

That you must not leave your baby's clothes outside after dark. Duppies will play with them, causing the infant's sleep to be disturbed.

* * * * * *

That if you let a baby cry at night, duppies will steal its voice.

* * * * * *

That you can stave off 'Rollin' Calf' with a pen knife.

If you meet this unwelcome spirit, take out your penknife, stick it in the ground and turn your back on him. Like a vampire can be held at bay with a crucifix, so this bull cannot advance on such a knife. You must then run home without looking back.

* * * * * *

That an event was recorded in the Gleaner newspaper, telling of a coffin that roamed around the streets of Kingston. This ominous apparition, with a John Crow bird riding on its lid, was witnessed by numerous citizens as it passed from house to house with no apparent means of propulsion. The incident caused large crowds to gather to view the macabre procession, but as the people arrived, the coffin had by some supernatural means, moved to another part of the city.

It was conjectured that the casket was on some mission to notify the householders where it paused, that a death was imminent within their family.

It has not been seen or heard of since.

The Great Train Crash

The Jamaican Railway was the first to be constructed in the British Colonies and was a private undertaking by two brothers, William and David Smith. These pioneers commenced construction on a line from Kingston to Spanish Town in September 1844, which was officially opened at Kingston Terminus the following year. This line was some fourteen miles long from Kingston to Angel, opening the 21st November 1845.

The company had a bumpy ride of progress due to the erratic rise and falls in the Sugar Industry, but economic development in 1860 led to an extension to Old Harbour from Spanish Town.

The JA Government took over in 1879 and further development led to the service from Kingston being extended all the way to Montego Bay. This line passed through Kendal in the Parish of Manchester where an appalling disaster took place described in this next tale.

****

The Holy Name Society attached to St. Anne's Roman Catholic Church in Western Kingston was contemplating a small outing to Montego Bay for Sunday 1st September 1957.

The diesel-electric locomotives were allocated to pull twelve coaches which had seating accommodation for 922 passengers, but by Saturday 31st August a thousand plus tickets had already been sold. A request was made for more carriages, but this was either ignored or overlooked.

On the Sunday morning a large crowd gathered and in spite of efforts by the police, they swarmed onto the platform and filled the train to overflowing, which left at 05.30 hours, carrying about 1,500 souls. More joined at Greenwich Town and Spanish Town making up to 1,800 passengers.

****

At the time of this tale a passenger train service ran right across the island of Jamaica, from Kingston to Montego Bay. Although there were some branch lines to stops like Frankfield, this route was the main artery of travel by rail. In no way, however, could the facility be described as an 'Express' because the engine and coaches had numerous stops on the way. There were two fast limited stop trains each day, but the everyday bustle of business was carried out on the slow trains. Children being carried to school. Higglers travelling to and from the markets. A baggage compartment was provided for them, but many preferred to sit in the carriage with their produce piled around them.

The occasional unofficial preacher would walk up and down the aisle, warning all in loud voice of the 'last coming' and the pickpockets had opportunities for rich pickings. Ice cream vendors sold their cones, cashew nut vendors their small and large bags of tasty crunchies and the railway company provided drinks, so all in all there was plenty of activity going on.

At the principal fruit selling districts vendors would be waiting on the platform, selling to the window passengers. There would be more than one occasion when the train left that a bunch of fruit would go in, but no money would come out.

Then there were the 'ratters,' who, because the train was so slow, would jump on for a free ride, leaping off again at the first sight of an inspector or ticket collector.

This busy business would go on for six days every week, but on the seventh day, like the Lord, there was rest, rest that is for all except the Express service and the occasional Sunday excursion.

The churches of the Roman Catholic faith annually arranged a convention in Montego Bay and members would travel in large numbers to enjoy this day out. Non-church members would take advantage of the transport to visit the seaside or to see relatives.

It was one of these Sundays in 1957, very early, that an engine and twelve coaches set off to Mo. Bay. Collecting more and more passengers all the way, it eventually arrived at Porus railway station, crammed to capacity, one could say to overflowing, as passengers, both legitimate and ratters, had already packed the carriages full and had spilled out to sit in the windows, hanging from the sides and doors, some even sitting on the train roof.

Louise, Victoria, Gwen and Diana Black had cooked up some rice and peas and chicken to pack in a basket with some cold drinks and they had stood on the platform since daybreak, but there was no room for them!

Louise cried bitterly.

When they arrived back home, Louise's mother Martha had tried to comfort her with:

"Every disappointment is for some good." Little did she know how prophetic was her attempt to pacify, but it was of no help to Louise. She was desperate to go.

****

We may assume that everyone enjoyed their day by the sea. It was very late as they made their weary way back to the station to set off for home, the coaches like sardine tins on wheels, packed once again with twice their load.

****

Then something awful happened at Kendal!

****

At 11.10 p.m. the train ran out of control on a steep mile long gradient and according to the enquiry that followed, attained a speed of 55 m.p.h., before the leading coach overturned to the right on a sharp left hand bend.

The subsequent examination of the wreckage pointed to "brake failure," due to an "accidental closing of an angle cock at the front end of the third coach," so that brakes were only functioning on the locomotives and the first two carriages. The brake power was therefore insufficient to hold the rest of the train. There was some suggestion that the valve had been tampered with by vandals riding the train. The opinion was that the driver was driving with due care and attention, but when he applied the brakes they just wouldn't hold.

Whatever was said at the enquiry about the cause of this catastrophe, the result was that the coaches left the engine and plunged down into a gully.

The carnage that followed was beyond belief.

The first carriage broke from its coupling with the engine, jumped the line and careered down the slope, pulling after it the others, one by one. As it rushed down into the gully, it rolled over to trap and crush scores of the screaming passengers and outside riders. The overcrowding inside caused bodies to be thrown together in a mass of flailing arms and legs. A few on the roof were luckily thrown clear but most of the window and side-riders were caught up and mangled, like sugar cane in a crusher, as the unit rolled over onto its side.

The second carriage plummeted down onto the first, splintering timbers flying in all directions, demolishing all in its path. Carriage after carriage came roaring down to smash one into another, cutting everyone down like a scythe cuts in a cornfield.

The last coach was the only one to survive with such relatively minimal damage that its occupants were virtually unscathed. These were the priests and nuns supervising the day trip, their survival being the source of ludicrous rumours that the church had taken the people off to be offered as sacrifice ..... whatever that was supposed to mean! Some superstitious elements of the population were afraid of the Papist religion, accusing it of idol worship and being practitioners of the Obeah.

Another rumour that was rife was that because thieves and pickpockets were exploiting the folks on the trip, God had decided to punish their wickedness. How strange that God would kill the majority to punish the minority!

Whatever the cause, be it human error or the intervention of God, the train crash killed, maimed and disfigured many many souls that day. One hundred and ninety persons were reported dead or missing and over one thousand were injured.

****

Louise was awakened early the following morning by the neighbours hoopin' up the lane, carrying the news:

"Train crash at Kendal."

After a hurried breakfast, Louise set off down the lane to school, but as she arrived in Porus where she normally caught a bus to go to the Camden College in May Pen, everyone was talking and gesticulating to each other about the terrible calamity. People were failing to turn up at their workplaces, preferring to go and witness the tragedy, so Louise joined the crowd by jumping on the back of a lorry heading towards Kendal.

When she arrived she regretted travelling to the scene to be a witness to such slaughter.

Crushed bodies lay everywhere, steel penetrating flesh and bone. Internal organs literally squeezed from chest and abdomen were splattered everywhere to be joined by hands, legs, arms and feet severed from their victims. Here and there a decapitation left a head mourning for its body.

Men, women, children and babies were shattered and scattered for all to see and the task of reuniting dismembered parts was a nauseating and grizzly task, as pieces were being placed into boxes for sorting later in a bizarre jigsaw of re-assembly.

The gully was red with blood.

One story that was told, was of a rescuer who thought he saw a wallet on the ground, whereupon he quickly and furtively snapped it up and slipped it into his back pocket. Later when he was advised that blood was spreading over the back of his trouser legs, he examined his pocket and was horrified to find a human hand.

88

How on earth did these rescue workers manage to cope with such a heart-rending task and deal with such slaughter. This was a national catastrophe.

****

Then the duppy stories started.

For many weeks to come eye witnesses testified to seeing headless, limbless or organless duppies fighting for their missing bits, crying and wailing:

[1] "Mi waan mi an!"
[2] "Mi waan mi yeye!"
[3] "Mi waan mi leg!"

Torsos deprived of their heads and therefore mouth and eyes, had difficulty calling out anything, so would blindly stumble from place to place, arms outstretched before them. Spectres of infants were seen lying where they had fallen, waving their poor little arms and legs in the air, and crying out pitifully for their mothers who would never come. Ghosts of men looking for lost wives, women looking for lost children. The tales were too numerous to tell.

****

An event occurred over and over during the following months, as Delroy, a local taxi driver will swear as true until his dying day.

He was out picking up passengers one dark night, when he was waved down by two well upholstered ladies, both of whom were dressed in their Sunday best dresses and hats. They declared their destination. Delroy declared the fare. With a nod the companions climbed into the back and off they went.

---

[1] "I want my hand."
[2] "I want my eye."
[3] "I want my leg."

The Great Train Crash

Delroy tried to strike up a conversation but he had no response from the pair, but did notice through his rear view mirror that the women just sat primly clutching their handbags, politely nodding and smiling as he chattered away.

The trip was not too long and they soon arrived at their yard. The ladies left the car, walked up the drive and entered the house.

Our taxi man sat for a moment assuming that they had perhaps gone inside to collect some money for the fare, but when they failed to re-emerge he gave three toots on the horn.

A moment later he was joined by an enquiring elderly gentleman requesting his business.

[4] "Mi waan mi fare."

[5] "Fare! wah fare?"

[6] "Mi waan mi fare from di two woman dem."

The householder listened to Delroy's story and when he heard the description of the plump couple he gasped out:

[7] "Dem de two woman eena mi sista dem. Dem ded ina di train crash."

Delroy fainted.

---

[4] "I want my fare."
[5] "Fare! What fare."
[6] "I want my fare from the two women."
[7] " Those two women are my sisters, they died in the train crash."

The Wager

Many a Jamaican enjoys a 'flutter'on the horses at the local betting shop. Then again, a wager on a football match might fit the bill, or a noisy session with the bone dice to divert hard earned money away from home. Notes can be exchanged over the card game 'Twenty-one' and the national pastime of dominoes can help to re-circulate currency. Donkey racing gives another opportunity to punters, as does the National Lottery, which is popular with both men and women alike. Most of the above are legal, but some folks will resort to 'under the counter' betting like 'Drop pan,' an unofficial lottery with numbers in bags that are sold on the streets by vendors or 'runners.' The Chinese also distribute bags containing 'seeds' for a lottery called Pik-a-pow.

* * * * * * *

This tale was narrated to me by my publisher, Mr Mike Henry.

* * * * * * *

Don and Earl were well known in the Belfield District.

Friendship was bonded by a mutual addiction to gambling, for they both seemed unable to resist a likely chance. Their favourite haunt was the local betting office, but one could rely on them to place a bet on anything, anywhere, anytime. There were occasions when they would even bet on whether the next person to turn the corner ahead of them would be a man or a woman. Sometimes they won, more often they lost, but in spite of the constant ear bending that they suffered from their good wives, they would frequently arrive home late at night having spent the rent or grocery money on some 'sure thing.'

Don and Earl were incorrigible.

This particular day, they had both suffered 'bad luck' in the betting shop, so they were drowning their sorrows in a popular bar, downing a few 'Red Stripes' and cursing the horses, the jockeys and the 'going'. Even the stable boys were at the receiving end of their anger, as nothing and no-one escaped their abuse.

A large brown cockroach ran across the rough wooden floor.

[1]"Bwoy" said Don. "Dat a di biggis cockroach mi eber si!"

Earl pondered for a moment, then declared:

[2]"Gweh man, wi ab bigga one dem inna mi yard."

[3]"Mi no tink so" retorted Don.

[4]"Mi seh mi hab man!" Earl was adamant and a bet was on.

The men arranged to meet at the bar on the following evening after having searched around for the largest roach that they each could find in their kitchens back home, but Don realised that his best option was to possess the monster that had scuttled across the bar, so he made a private arrangement with the barkeeper to stay in his dark premises that night, on a vigil to catch his favourite contender. This he did, lantern at the ready, until the brown beauty fell into his clutches.

They met as agreed and as they peeped into the jars it was clear that Don was an easy winner, so Earl paid his debt to the accompaniment of jeering and laughter from the regular customers, then sat brooding over his misfortune.

Not for long, however, because as a twinkle returned to his eye he turned to his friend maintaining that:

[5]"Fi yu mite be bigga, but mi a bet yu seh fi mi faster dan fi yu." Oh dear! Another bet was on the way.

The drinking fraternity loved to watch these cronies vying to win the upper hand and they knew what was afoot, so they all set

---

[1] "Boy! That's the biggest cockroach I've ever seen!"
[2] "Go away man, we have bigger ones than that in my house".
[3] "I don't think so!"
[4] "I say I have man!"
[5] "Yours might be bigger, but I bet you that mine's faster!"

to, following the instructions as Earl asked for two chalk circles to be marked out on the floor.

First, a small one to hold the two jars, which were placed neck down onto the deck to contain the 'runners;' then a ring some six feet in diameter. The first across this second chalk mark would be the victor. All of the lads were getting in on the action, noisily laying side bets on the contenders, but as the bartender stepped forward with arm raised, holding a cloth that would indicate the start of the race when it hit the floor, a hush descended on the gathering.

It seemed to take an eternity to flutter down, but then the jars were up and they were off.. What a clatter ensued!

The men were down on their knees, banging with anything that came to hand, to drive the opposition back from the winning line. The sound of rattle, bang and wallop carried to the road outside, drawing a crowd of shouting supporters who caroused around the door, many of whom having no idea what they were hollering about. The pandemonium reached a climax when Don's cockroach, which had just run in two circles, suddenly came to a halt, sat quite still for a reflective moment, then shot away at breakneck speed to make itself an easy winner. So now it was the largest AND the quickest!

Earl groaned and turned back to his drink. [6]"Mek wi dun now. Yuh laas too much moni areddy" chided Don.

[7] "Mi hab wan adder bet weh yu cyaan win," crowed Earl.
[8] "Wha yu a tark 'bout?"

[9] "Mi bet yu, yu cyaan walk tru di cemetry a nite time!" challenged Earl.

Don's 'head raised' with fright at the very thought. He had been brought up to fear the night duppies and a cemetery would be the very last place that you would find him after dark. Earl had really hit the mark with his wager and he knew it, so he taunted his friend over and over again with his alarming chal-

---

[6] "Let's finish now! You've lost too much money already."
[7] "I have another bet that you can't win!"
[8] "What are you talking about?"
[9] "I'll bet you can't walk through the cemetery at night!"

lenge.

The lads in the bar joined in to torment Don and egg him on to take up the gauntlet. It was only the high level of alcohol in his blood stream that eventually persuaded him to yield and take the risk.

So arrangements were made for our contenders to meet the following night at the bar and just before midnight, accompanied by their witnesses, they made their way to the cemetery. Everyone had turned up as agreed and they commenced to lay down the ground rules for the ordeal which was to follow:

Firstly, Don had to start at the main gate and walk right through the centre of the burial ground to the rear of the plot. The witnesses were to verify that he had passed from wall to wall and that he was not accompanied. Not that anyone would go with him anyway. To verify that he had indeed passed through the midst of the sepulchres, he was to carry a wooden mallet and a metal tipped stake, that was to be driven into a named tomb situated at the midpoint of the journey, to be corroborated the next day.

All of the umpires took up their positions, then Don was led grudgingly to the main gate and encouraged to enter. As the hinged iron barrier closed behind him, a not so stout hearted gambler weighed the possibility of a retraction. It was so ominously dark and menacing that he froze for a moment and he became aware of the sweat on his forehead. He carried a lantern to light the way, which was raised high to kindle some courage, but with little effect. Ghostly white tombstones seemed to spread endlessly out before him, waiting to introduce him to their long deceased inhabitants. Shakily, he wandered between row upon row of old collapsing graves, looking for the specific stone where he was to leave the marker. Suddenly something flew past his head that might have only been a foraging bat, but Don created all sorts of monsters to account for the intrusion. He was sweating profusely and the panic welled up inside his breast, so he sighed with some relief when he found the designated sepulchre, for then he knew that his trial was half over. All he was required to do now was to leave the marker, then escape this fearful place in a hurry. Hastily, he placed the stake on the tomb stone, giving it a mighty blow with the mallet, which having completed its task was impetuously cast away. Now he could make his way to safety, but as he took his first nervous step away from the burial place, something held him fast. Gripped with terror, he endeavoured to move away, but yet again something or someone was holding onto his coat tail. He daren't look behind him, dreading that he was held by some ghastly resident of this ghostly housing estate.

[10] "Lawd a massy. Im get mi!" he croaked.

A terrible pain struck him in the chest and he dropped stone dead.

When he failed to make his exit, his friends assumed that he must have taken fright and left for home by vaulting over the perimeter wall. No-one volunteered a search to find out otherwise.

The next day, when it was discovered that Don had not returned home from the ordeal, his mates came a-searching, to find him dead and stiff. They probed the scene for a probable cause for this tragedy, but no theory was forthcoming.

Another mystery that was never solved, was a question raised by one bystander who asked:

[11] "Wah mek im peg down im coat pan de tomb?"

---

[10] "Lord have mercy He's got me!"
[11] "What made him peg down his coat on the tomb?"

The Saintly Duppy

This story was told to me by Maas Alvan Anthony Ebanks. He's proud of his full name.

Maas Alvan is the husband of aunt Winnie who in turn is the cousin of Leonie, my wife and they both live on Acre Street in a house up the lane, at the bottom of which stands the Redberry Church of the Nazarene.

Like many folks in this district Alvan puts food on the table by farming (some twenty acres or more of land), cultivating yam, sweet potato, pineapple and banana, and has coconut trees, ackee, orange, limes, lemons, sweet sop, sour sop, tangerine and other trees I can't remember. He rears cows, pigs, goats and chickens and I can picture him now, machete in hand wandering in his kingdom, reaping the harvest.

Whenever one visits the Ebanks domain, you will find a welcome and will be offered oranges or a 'jelly' (coconut).

By and large I find the rural people of Jamaica, those who work the land, most hospitable and generous and they are willing to share what they have, giving thanks to the Lord.

The Saintly Duppy is a tale that reflects Maas Alvan's personality.

****

A man was desperately lost in a wilderness.

He had been lost for many days, his situation now being most dire as he was totally out of water and had only one last banana to eat.

His spirit had already given up the fight and he wished to

The Saintly Duppy

take his own life. So spying a solitary palm tree, he climbed up to the top and sat, legs straddled amongst the leaves. He slowly peeled his fruit and threw the skin to the ground.

He took his time ruminating over his last meal and his last act, whilst looking down to see how far he had to fall to end his life. He had calculated that the best way to fall to solve his problem would be to strike the ground with his head, so he positioned himself for a swan dive. His concentration was diverted by a cracking of twigs in the undergrowth down below.

A man, seemingly in a worse state that himself, dishevelled and travel weary, staggered towards the foot of the tree, pounced on the banana skin, gobbled it up, then staggered off on his hopeless journey.

Staring down in wonderment, he thought that if a man in a more calamitous state than himself could battle on and struggle to survive, then so could he. He climbed down and started out after the stranger, but no way could he catch him up. He called out, but no answer. From time to time this man that he'd never met before, would beckon to invite him to follow.

Soon he entered scrubby bushes and was lost to view, so the desperate man followed and struggled to pass through the clump of shrubs, finding himself in a clearing. The stranger had vanished but he had been led to a small village.

Tottering to the nearest house, he was met on the porch by the owner who after a brief conversation invited him in for a meal and a drink. The occupant proposed that if he was prepared to do the menial tasks around the house, he could have free board and lodgings in return. Of course it was an offer too good to refuse and certainly a better state than starving in the wilderness. So he swept the yard, cleaned the house, tended the chickens and slept in the shed, working so diligently that the house owner eventually started to give him a small wage.

So he progressed, working and saving his small income. He was such a good worker that others in the village started to call, inviting him to work on their piece of land or to do simple labouring tasks.

He prospered, building a small roadside shop which was well

supported by the local population. His reputation spread far and wide and soon his business had grown into a large wholesale and retail store and he became a wealthy man.

During all this prosperous lifetime, he never forgot the stranger who saved his life in the wilderness.

He lived to a ripe old age, marrying and being the father of eight children and fifteen grandchildren, so when his time came to pass over he lay on his bed surrounded by a large gathering of family, friends and neighbours.

As he lay there, he began to reminisce about his life events and was telling his story of his lucky encounter with the starving man all those years before.

Everyone of his friends and neighbours nodded and smiled as he told his tale, then one came forward to explain to the store-keeper that the 'saint' who had saved him was well known to all. He was a man who had died long before the attempted suicide and was spending his spirit existence helping people in distress.

He lay for a moment contemplating this revelation, when his attention was drawn to the window by a movement and there, standing outside on the porch, he could see the man who often visited him in his dreams.

It was his saviour of long ago, still as dishevelled, but smiling ..... oh! such a wonderful smile ..... and beckoning!

He closed his eyes.

When he opened them again he was standing on the veranda beside his good friend, the saintly duppy.

Glancing through the window into the bedroom, he saw the gathering around his death bed. His spirit had left his body and was waiting to journey to the other side.

Waving goodbye and turning around, he walked with his companion into the 'light', leaving his family and his many friends to celebrate his life and mourn his passing.

Mr. Talaman

You will find large community cemeteries here and there in Jamaica. I prefer burial in the grounds of your own yard, that is the long standing custom in most rural areas, even today. There is something comforting about having your parents, grandparents and other family members buried close to the location where they lived out their lives and gave their time and experience to continue the family traditions. Every year when my wife and I fly over to visit friends and surviving relatives, we set time aside to paint the sepulchres on the family plot and have some quiet time to talk to Leonie's dear departed.

This traditional tale tells of such a bonded family, both living and deceased, who were far too keen to help each other as they went about their day to day business,

* * * * * * *

Ezra Talaman lived with his dear wife Shernette and their two young sons in a basic residence, located in the bush surrounding the community of Mocho in Clarendon. They had come by this property when an uncle had passed over and as they appeared to be his nearest surviving relatives they had moved into this ramshackle dwelling and were making every effort to improve the estate. They were favoured with some six or seven acres of fertile land which Ezra had nurtured during their two years occupancy, so that it was now offering a variety of crops that kept hunger at bay. Shernette higgled in May Pen to sell this harvest and by and large they were satisfied. At any rate they didn't starve.

Whilst his wife was vending, Ezra had plenty to do to keep

101

him out of mischief. Not only did he cultivate his crops, he also had to keep a paternal eye on the children who were not yet old enough for school. One day he was working very hard to clear a particularly stubborn section of land that he had decided would be ideal for sowing corn, when he was approached by a friendly man.

[1] "Wah yu a do?"

[2] "Mi a bush di lan fi sow carn," answered Ezra.

The stranger turned on his heels, strolled down to the family burial plot and standing on a sepulchre, he cried out:

"Big and lickle, lickle and big. Cum 'elp Missa Talaman bush lan."

A silence of anticipation fell all around as the creatures of the bush watched and waited for some response to this appeal. Then the duppies began to awaken from their slumbers, and slowly they rose from their coffins to join their companion.

Poor Ezra keeled over with fear, passing out and not returning to his senses until his children shook him to consciousness some two hours later, when he found that all of the land had been cleared and was ready for sowing. There was no sign of the ghostly farmers.

That night Shernette listened with amusement to her husband babbling some tale of spectres and uninvited visitors.

She sniffed his breath for a tell tale hint of rum and wondered why her usually down to earth husband had suddenly developed such a vivid imagination. She thought that he had worked hard on the land, however, so she gave him a hug and consoled him with some 'bed wuk' that night.

Our good wife set out early the next day, as was her custom, carrying produce on her head for sale in May Pen. Ezra set to cutting up dead timber for the wood stove.

He had been sawing and chopping for a good half hour when the stranger of yesterday called out, wanting to know what he was doing. Dropping the axe, Ezra ran to the house porch ready

---

[1] "What are you doing?"
[2] "I'm clearing the land to sow corn!"

to take cover behind a closed door. The man called after him, to assure him that no harm was intended. His smile seemed so genuine that Ezra cautiously stepped back into the yard to reply: [3] "Mi a chap wood fi di fire."

Ezra watched with growing alarm and fear, as the intruder headed towards the graves yet again. "Big and lickle, lickle and big. Cum 'elp Missa Talaman chap wood."

Ezra knew what the next sequence of events would be, so he shot back onto the veranda, dashed into the house, bolting the door behind him and took up a vantage position at the window facing the cemetery. As he expected the dead rose up from their rest, to begin sawing and chopping up the fire wood. Unfortunately, not only did they cut the dead timber, but they felled all of the fruiting trees and reduced them to kindling as well.

Mister Talaman was quite powerless to stop this rape of his land, never having been taught anti-duppy magic, so you can imagine what a difficult task he had to explain to his wife how their fruitful ackee, orange, grapefruit and banana trees had been decimated in her absence. I'm afraid that he was on the receiving end of a few well chosen 'rass' words of wisdom that night.

It was with great trepidation that farmer Talaman stepped down from the porch the following morning furtively looking for the stranger, but there was no sign of man or duppy. With a sigh of relief he called the boys from the house, then set about his chores for the day. All was going well, when some conflict arose between the children that led to screaming, fisticuffs and tears. Ezra took up a switch and proceeded to reprimand his offspring, but this only led to more commotion and he became more and more angry.

"Wah yu a do?"

A now familiar voice questioned the activity, but the father was so frustrated with his children that he failed to recognise his visitor, so without turning around he continued with his disciplinary duties, shouting out:

---

[3] "I'm chopping wood for the fire!"

[4]"Di bwoy dem a mek too much nize, so mi a beat dem!" Our kind hearted visitor went straightway to fetch his friends.

"Big and lickle, lickle and big. Cum 'elp Missa Talaman beat di bwoy dem."

Young Joshua had run indoors to escape the wrath of his father, but his poor brother was still outside when the duppies arrived, armed with sticks to help Missa Talaman with his admonition.

The misguided spectres set to with a will, screaming with delight as they laid into their victim. They thrashed him, they hammered him, they flailed him, they flogged him and beat him until the poor mite was dead.

Poor Ezra could only stand helpless and horror-struck, as he watched his boy being whipped to death.

It was a painful and difficult month that followed. Shernette was absolutely distraught with grief and the funeral was plagued with rumours concerning the strange circumstances surrounding the boy's untimely departure. The police made periodic visits to investigate the possibility of criminal proceedings, but eventually the Talamans were able to return to growing and selling what was left of their meagre crops. Shernette was back at the market and Ezra pottered about on his land.

When the time came for Joshua to be washed, his father brought out a tin bath, filled it with cold water, then placed it in the sun to warm up

"Wah yu a do?"

"Go weh! Go weh! wailed Ezra. "Yu kill mi pickney!"

[5a] "Wah yu a bex fah?" the stranger pleaded. [5b] "Afta a no mi kill di bwoy, a di duppy dem kill im!"

[6] "Go weh and mek mi warm up mi pickney baat wata!"

Our stranger sets off to the cemetery yet again.

"Big and lickle, lickle and big. Cum 'elp Missa Talaman bathe de bwoy."

---

[4] "The children are making too much noise, so I'm giving them a beating!"
[5a] "Why are you vexed?"
[5b] "It's not me that killed the boy, the duppies killed him."
[6] "Go away and let me warm up the child's bath water!"

The duppies were swift to respond to the call, for they enjoyed playing about with children's bath water, as is their nature. Whilst two duppies removed young Joshua's clothes and placed him in the tub, others lit a fire to boil up water in an old kerosene can. As it boiled, they poured it into the bath, scalding the poor Talaman boy to death.

The duppies danced around with glee, shouting:

[7] "Lawd, the wata sweet 'im so, till im 'kin im teet."

****

Author's comment: The patois ' to kin im teet' or 'to skin his teeth,' basically means to smile, but here refers to the macabre expression that looked like a grin appearing on the boy's face as he was scalded. As he grimaced with the intense heat, his mouth would draw back to reveal his teeth.

---

[7] "He likes the water so much that he's smiling."

Buried Treasure

How many of you are old enough to remember the golden era of cinema?

I remember most clearly going to the local 'tupenny rush' Picture Palace when I was a boy, to see Errol Flynn and Tyrone Power in those exciting swashbuckling films about the pirates and privateers who roamed the Caribbean seas, robbing and looting the ships that crossed their path. Or Treasure Island, with one legged Long John Silver and Black Spot and the search for a buried treasure. I would sword fight with imaginary adversaries, all the way home from the Lenos Picture Palace crying out with the occasional "Have at you!" and dodging in and out to avoid deriding pedestrians and Bluebeard the pirate.

Do you recall the larger than life character, Captain Henry Morgan?

This incorrigible rogue was an opportunist privateer, who was given authority by the Governor of Jamaica to fight the Spanish, taking the booty as pay for his services. Morgan more than held his own with the ruffians of the day and was so successful with his raids on Spanish ports that he was knighted in 1675 by King Charles II. These exploits took him far afield, but he always returned 'home' to Port Royal in Jamaica , where he later became Deputy Governor. All of this activity made him a wealthy man, who spent his twilight years as a plantation owner. I wonder if he kept his money in the bank?

Unfortunately, much of the colourful history of Port Royal that was captured in those old films, was swept away by a mighty earthquake in 1696.

I wondered where Morgan kept his money, because I remember scenes when the pirate captain Bluebeard, would carry great trunks from his ship, that were full of jewels and Spanish gold doubloons, to be secretly buried on some remote island. The secret was always well kept, because the seamen who laboured to carry and dig the hole, would then be summarily killed and buried with the treasure and 'dead men tell no tales.'

Before this time, the Spanish were a powerful nation in Jamaica, who since its discovery by Columbus in 1494 had governed the island for a century and a half until it fell to the British in 1655. During these one hundred and sixty one years, however, tales were told (which still persist to this day), of Spanish jars. It would seem that during these days of raiders from the sea, the Spaniards would hide their valuables and money in pottery jars, which would then be buried under the roots of some tree that grew in an easily remembered location. The practice was to have the slave who dug the hole killed and buried close to the site so that this poor soul's duppy would guard the hoard. Some of the owners were killed by the aforesaid marauders, so some jars are said to be still buried, awaiting those courageous treasure hunters who would dare to risk a confrontation with the guardian duppy.

The following amusing story, told by a member of the family, has undertones of these old tales of buried treasure.

* * * * * * *

It was the 24th of May in 1948 when Benjamin Brown made his way towards the docks in Kingston harbour.

He had read an article in the national Jamaican press, that a journey to the British Isles was on offer to ex-service men and women on the steamship Empire Windrush, at a price that many could afford. The economy was not good at home and it was rumoured that there was work aplenty in England. Since he had returned home from serving his king and country he had fallen on hard times. Here was a chance to improve himself!

So it was that the retired troopship left the harbour carrying four hundred and ninety two intrepid souls, who were searching for a better life in foreign climes, but having no idea what was awaiting them. Little did they know of the tribulations and insults that were just around the corner.

Time passed by and they endured the overcrowded conditions on board, comforted with thoughts of the streets that were paved with gold.

When Benjamin stepped ashore at Tilbury, it was to a cool reception. There had been some political rumblings about sending them all back to Jamaica, but thanks to a resident fellow West Indian intervening on their behalf, two hundred and thirty five of his comrades and himself, had at least some protection from the weather, albeit in an old communal air raid shelter on Clapham Common. There was work to be found and Benjamin was soon collecting fares on a public transport bus, but accommodation was a different matter. He would walk the streets for hour after hour, knocking on doors, to be always informed that there was 'no room in the inn.' Signs would be placed in bed and breakfast pub windows saying "No coloureds, No Irish, No dogs," but eventually he found a single room bed sit, with everything shared, let to him by an Asian landlord.

Mr. Brown, like many Jamaicans, was a proud man, so he worked and saved until he was able to put a down payment on a little 'two up and two down' house, that had an outside toilet across the yard.

By 1964, things were really looking up! He had married and was raising two delightful daughters. They had all moved a little more upmarket and were now living in a semi-detached house in a more agreeable area of town, but his roots in Jamaica were never far from his mind. Every so often they would return to visit family in the land of 'wood and water' and he had promised his wife that when they retired, they would return to Jamaica and build a retirement house on a plot of family land that awaited their home coming.

So they continued to work and save hard.

One old fashioned custom, however, never left our intrepid immigrant. He had a strange suspicion of banks, preferring to keep his savings in a small locked box that was hidden under a

108

loose floorboard in the box room of the house. He had quite a stash of ten pound notes, all waiting to make his retirement comfortable and secure. This hiding place was his idea of safety, but the little nest egg would have been quite a windfall for some enterprising burglar.

The time was now rapidly approaching for him to set in motion the preparing of his parcel of land back home, so he arranged for five weeks of extended leave, packed his money box in the bottom of his travel bag, kissed his wife and set off to begin his life's ambition.

His flight was uneventful, his brother meeting him at Norman Manley Airport in Kingston and soon he was hugging up his relatives. A few days to socialise and he was all ready to set about the business of beginning the '3 Bedroom, Living/Dining Room, Air-conditioned, Fully Grilled Windows/Doors on 3 Acres of Fruited Land.'

His prime task was to lay the footings for the solid foundation of the main building that he would erect on his next visit. Negotiating a going price with some of the local boys, work was soon under way, digging the trenches, pouring the concrete as a solid base for his home and seating in the first layer of blocks and steel that would resist the fiercest of hurricanes. Ben supervised the labour, to ensure that there were not too many chat and joke breaks and things went very well. He paid off the workers and began to prepare for the flight home, but when the time came for him to pack his suitcase, he thought it might be a good idea to leave his money box somewhere safe, where it could await his next building trip. The following day he set out with box and spade to bury his hard earned savings somewhere on his few acres, checking carefully around to make sure that he had no uninvited callers. All was clear, so he dug a deep hole near a mango tree and buried the wooden casket, money and all. To be sure that he would have no problem finding the cache the following year, he took a photograph of the spot with his old Baby Brownie camera.

Back home in Blighty he was glad to receive a rotund hug from his dear wife, then he brought out the presents that he had purchased at Kingston Market, along with the bammy, sour sop and other goodies that would be appreciated. They all had a pleasant evening at home, talking about the news from the old country.

The following day Benjamin took his reel of holiday film to Boots the Chemists for developing and four days later he stood with an envelope of pictures clasped in his hands. Being too impatient to wait to enjoy them, he sat on a bench near the open market to browse the memories. With the occasional chuckle he fingered through the snaps, until with a grunt of approval, he held the image of the mango tree on his piece of land. He was about to slip it back amongst the others, when something in the foliage caught his eye and peering closer he saw to his horror that a young man was sitting in the tree branches, smiling in triumph.

Mr Brown immediately knew that his life savings were lost and with a cry of despair he fell dead to the ground.

The story didn't end there, however, for let it be known to all those who seek encounters with the spirits of the dead, that there is a mango tree somewhere in Jamaica, that is visited every night by a wailing duppy, who digs furiously to find a box full of ten pound notes.

IT DIGS IN VAIN!

Rollin' Calf and Hoopin' Bwoy

Jonkunoo is a Festival that was once a regular part of Christmas and New Year Celebrations in Jamaica, but seems to be dying out, particularly in the rural areas.

It is an honourable memorial to John Conny who was a leader of the Black Traders near Axim, Guinea, active in 1720 AD.

Sometimes spelt as John Canoe, this dance festival was allowed by the plantation owners during slavery times. Jonkunoo is an African 'Ewe' language word meaning Sorcerer man or Witch Doctor.

The principal dancers, who are mainly comprised of men are the King, Queen, Kuku or Actorboy, Pitchy- Patchy, Horsehead, Cowhead, Devil and Mother Lundi. The characters bear a strange resemblance to those found in the Mummer's Play, still performed in England. The name may have been modified to John Canoe, because one of the principal dancers carried a boat headress that looked like a canoe.

This story introduces the reader to two supernatural characters:

(i) Rollin' Calf, who is a duppy bull that appears to revellers during the haunting hours of night, especially after they've consumed good Jamaican Rum.

(ii) Hoopin' Bwoy is a spectre who is often heard at the time that Rollin' Calf is out and about. Backgrounds seem scanty, but some say he is the calf's drover, thus his cry of "ooop, back!" Others say he is the duppy of a trustee slave who was in charge of other slaves and was allowed to carry a whip to maintain order. Yet others say that one cannot look upon Hoopin' Bwoy and live, so all in all an encounter to be avoided.

111

Jonkunoo

I have just spent two hours, from eleven until one o'clock in the morning at our Baptist church on New Years Eve at the Watch Night Service.

Now it's time for the old time revelry of Jonkunoo, and folks are coming onto the streets, some with the skulls of horses on their heads. The African style drumming begins and we are dancing wildly to the chanting of:

"Thank God to see another New Year morning.

We wish you a Happy New Year."

Christianity and ancient folk lore are married in a strange fusion of activities.

In the light of the home made torches I can see mamma, with my sister Gwen being dragged behind, pushing through the crowd to get home.

[1] "No 'ab nuttin fi do wi de Pagan dem." she cries to me and little sister sobs in fear of the frightful heads, clapping teeth and white faces in the torch light.

'Horsing' up and down with the other revellers, I pop into the bars to keep topping up with beer and the occasional shot of rum, whilst the carnival is going on and on into the early hours.

I'm tiring now and I've certainly had too much to drink, so I weave away, setting off on the long walk home leaving the sound of drums and dancing behind.

I stop suddenly, straining to hear a sound coming from deep in the bush over to my left:

"Ooop. Ooop ... back! Ooop. Ooop ... back!"

I hope that's not what I think it is.

"Ooop. Ooop ... back!" ..... over to my right.

My legs begin to buckle and I sober up rather quickly

"Ooop. Ooop ... back!" now the calling is coming from behind, back down the lane.

It must be Hoopin' Bwoy, so I tell my legs not to let me down, quicken up my pace and kiss the crucifix that I keep on a gold chain round my neck. I walk at quite a pace for some distance, then I stop still and listen to hear whether I'm being followed. All has gone quiet. So far so good.

---

[1] "Don't have anything to do with the Pagans."

Then coming up behind I hear a snorting and snuffling sound and a quick glance over the shoulder reveals a dark shape in the gloom of the shadows cast by the trees at the roadside. I spin around to be faced by Rollin' Calf himself, the ghostly bull that mamma had threatened me with when I was a child and was naughty and stayed out late. It stands in the middle of the lane, large head shaking from side to side, his enormous horns flashing in the moonlight, and his eyes all afire, dripping red to the ground. He paws the road with his hooves, striking sparks into the air. Then he charges straight at me. Not waiting for an introduction I turn on my heels and run as fast as my bare feet will carry me.

"I must get to the cross-roads, must make the cross-roads."

Mamma used to tell me that if I'm chased by Rollin' Calf, I should get to a cross-road and quickly hide, because when this ghastly bull reaches the intersection it becomes confused, not knowing which way to go. There are no cross-roads near so I must use another trick that pappa told me.

Fumbling in my pocket for a box of matches, I strike one and throw it to the ground, take a second, strike it and throw it to the ground, (remember I'm running all the while), strike a third and PRETEND to throw it to the ground. Leaping into the bush, I hide behind a tree and watch an unfolding scene.

Now Rollin' Calf finds the first match, snuffles around for the second, then bellows with rage when it cannot find the third. He cannot follow me until he finds the third match, which is now safely hidden in my pocket, so I quietly slip away to continue on my journey.

I smile in triumph.

"Ooop. Ooop ... back!"

As I turn a bend in the road I come face to face with Hoopin' Bwoy.

I look him straight in the eye!

He looks straight back at me,

..... and I die of fright!

Now that I'm a duppy, I'll wait for you tomorrow night in the moonlight. You'll know that it's me because I'll call out:

"Coo-ee. Coo-ee."

114

Rollin' Calf and Hoopin' Bwoy

The Alligator

This is the first of two stories told to me by Roy Jones, known in Mother Bryant Hill and around the district as 'Spoogy.'

Roy is a grand chap and husband to his lovely wife, Doreen. They have two gorgeous daughters, Janeal and Fitara, a son Rohan and a grand son Jason.

Three years ago Roy was working as a fruit picker in the district of Peru, Burlington, Vermont, U.S.A., when he fell from a tree, breaking his neck and is now paralysed from the mid-chest down. He has become a prisoner in a wheel chair in his own home.

Is he downhearted? Not a bit. He remains the mischievous rascal that his stories highlight and his yard is the place to visit if you need cheering up. I remember well the twinkle in his eye when he narrated these tales of a duppy alligator and Trick and a Treat.

* * * * * * *

When I was a young man of nineteen years, I walked to a place called Harmonds district looking for my girlfriend. It was starting to get dark, so I wasn't too keen to be out because I had a great fear of duppies. Mind you, the pull of a girl could be stronger than the fear of a ghost.

It was later when I was walking back home that my thoughts wandered back to duppies because it was just the night for them to visit, everything being flooded with clear bright moonlight. Everywhere the shadows from the bush danced and shimmered

116

on the road. It was dry and clear, but unbeknown to me, further up the road closer to home, it had been raining heavily.

The track was very rough and full of potholes, so I had to take care to avoid tripping and stumbling. Looking ahead up a long straight stretch, I noticed some distance away, an alligator lying in the middle of the road. What an alligator was doing in these parts I couldn't imagine, but it was there all right, as clear as could be, a long dark figure in the moonlight facing towards me and blocking my path.

Mamma had warned me that if one met an alligator at night it could well be a duppy in disguise, so I stood still for a while to consider my options.

I could turn around and walk back to take refuge with my girlfriend. What reason could I give her for my return? I certainly wasn't going to make a fool of myself by admitting to her my duppy phobia.

The second option would be to head into the bush and circle around to get the other side of the alligator and make my way safely home from there, but there were dangers in this too. This thick bush could be tricky to manoeuvre in the dark and there might be other unearthly monsters waiting in the undergrowth.

The third plan would be to just run like fire past the alligator, but no way was I going to take such a chance, so I decided on this last line of action.

My Mother once told me that if I was faced by such a situation, there was an anti-duppy ritual that might work in my favour.

(There are endless magical rituals to ward off these creatures).

I was to bite my thumb, then my index finger, then my middle finger, then my third finger and finally my little finger on my left hand and then repeat the ritual on my right hand thumb and fingers. After completing this cycle I was then to throw a rock to strike the alligator right behind his head and this should drive the duppy away.

I stood trembling on the road, facing my fear, but also thinking that if I didn't pluck up some courage soon I'd be here 'til daybreak. Ah! Yes! Option five was to just stay where I was 'til

The Alligator

daybreak, when the early rising sun would drive the spirit away, but what shame in not overcoming this fear.

Taking in a deep breath I bit thumb, finger, finger, finger, finger, thumb, finger, finger, finger, finger and picking up a rock I hurled it with all my strength at the alligator. It bounced on the road a good five feet this side of the wicked duppy, but it never flinched.

I tried again, thumb, finger, finger ... oh! you know the routine - threw another rock - missed by a mile!

I realised I might be too far away for a good accurate throw, so I drew a little closer (not too close mind), but my accuracy didn't improve as I was still shaking with anxiety. I threw rock after rock to no avail. The reptile just would not leave. For a whole hour, I threw stone after stone but the darned thing wouldn't move an inch.

I was starting to get angry at myself now, thinking how foolish it would seem to my friends when they heard I'd been throwing stones at a duppy all night.

This was it, my last chance. I knew now that my only likelihood of victory was a full blow with a stone on its back, so I looked around for the largest rock I could find. Here was one, heavy and jagged. I could just about lift it with both hands.

Here we go again. Bite my thumb, finger, finger, finger, finger, thumb, finger, finger, finger, finger, and with a grunt I hoisted the rock above my head and started to stagger towards the duppy. Steady now, I must get as close as possible. Closer, closer, closer until it was right before me. I took two more steps until my legs seemed to be astride its ominous head, then with a yell and a great heave I cast the rock down on the black shimmering back.

SPLASH! A fountain of water rose up and drenched me from head to foot.

The alligator was just an illusion caused by moonlight shining on a pot hole that was filled with water.

I'll tell you this though, I've never been frightened of duppies since!

119

Duppy Mellow and the Mangoes

This is a favourite story told by Auntie Winnie and Leonie.

****

Our home was an old colonial style house with a porch all around, that couldn't be seen because it was situated back from the road in Redberry. There was a wood-fire kitchen a step from the house and we had our own water supply in a tank, with its own catchment barbecue slope on which we used to dry coffee, corn and the like. Mind you if there was a sudden downpour of rain, we would all have to rush out to prevent the beans being swept down into the container.

The track passing our house was used as a busy short-cut to Dawkins District. People would just drop in and knowing Martha my mother, they were sure to be fed and served drinks. As a child, I remember many a telling off because some pernickety old lady visitor would complain when a drinking glass was not presented just so.

Martha would listen to all of the gossip, but was known for her discretion, her good advice and sympathy. She was always ready to offer local remedies to ailing friends. Dandelion coffee for kidney trouble, jointer bush to put in the bath for arthritis and she would gather different herbs from the bush herself every week to boil up a tonic.

Mamma was wise in the old ways, but also forward thinking

and modern, particularly for her children, who were encouraged to strive for betterment. This was her message to all.

Martha was tall, certainly as tall as Sharlotte and very well built and buxom. Her skin was very dark and she had strong black hair, which she inherited from her African mother. She had a large nose that we all talked about and thick generous lips. Her father was of mixed (possibly Scottish and Negro) race and Martha inherited the most unusual watery pale blue eyes.

She had no teeth, as these were all extracted in her early forties, but would only wear her dentures when out visiting, removing them whilst she ate, placing them in her handkerchief. She was told on numerous occasions that her false teeth were provided to help her to eat her food but she would not be told. Mamma had her ways and would not be swayed.

She worked hard all her life, putting her hands to anything that would place food on the table and educate her daughters. Cultivating her land, rearing her family and animals, higgling on the Porus road or at Mandeville Market and being prepared to work all hours, six days a week.

On the day of this tale, Martha was sitting in the doorway to the kitchen, dressed in one of her simple cotton floral dresses, with a full apron that covered most of her dress other than the sleeves and back. Her hands were thrust into the two long pouchy pockets let into the apron front. She had a 'tie-head' scarf covering her hair and her bare black feet were both planted solidly on the ground. In her mouth she held a chalk pipe firmly between her gums, puffing away at the tobacco that she grew in her yard.

She was waiting for Sharlotte, who was coming down to stay over, so that they could make an early start to pick mangoes, up Acre Street, that they intended to sell at Kendal.

Sharlotte strolled into the yard carrying a basket, so was prepared to collect the fruit the following morning. She was Martha's niece, sister Sarah's only daughter. She was tall like her Aunt but so very thin. She'd always been the same. Sharlotte had strong long black hair that grew to the nape of the neck and displayed her usual smile, sporting beautiful white teeth. She only lived up the road, but this couple enjoyed each other's company, so often stayed over as aunts and nieces who love each other are delighted to so do.

They wanted an early start in the morning because it was a long walk to Kendal, where the demand for mangoes was good. Having no clock, however, they were both awake much earlier than intended, but as they were up they agreed that they might as well proceed to the fruit trees.

It was still bright moonlight and Martha walked ahead of Sharlotte who was cold, huddled up and walking more slowly. Martha had passed Dawkins Gate, where Mrs. Dora Mellow now lived in a house on the left, close to the road. Her husband had died three years before and Sharlotte had known him well.

As Sharlotte trudged on she became aware of movement under the mango trees that were close to the road on widow Mellow's land. She saw a figure standing directly beneath one of the trees, so hurried her pace, thinking that it was Martha who had stopped to allow her to catch up, but as she drew closer she realised it was a man, a tall very black man, dressed in a brown shirt, black pants and shoes. Over one arm he carried a basket which Sharlotte recognised. It was obviously old and battered, looking as if it had been through the wars, (as they would say *creng-creng*), it being held together with tied around wire.

"Lawd!" said Sharlotte, as she realised the basket belonged to Maas Mellow. Standing quite still, her 'just out of bed' cold turned into an icy feeling that bit deep into her bones, but she quickly threw this off when she realised that she had no fear of this duppy; just a fascination for Maas Mellow as he went about his business.

She watched with curiosity aroused, as he began to pick up mangoes off the ground. Each time he gathered one, he would place it carefully in the basket, then spin around three times before picking up another. He performed this little dance ritual three times for three mangoes, real mangoes that now sat snugly in his basket.

Sharlotte called up the road for Martha to come witness this moonlit spectacle, but auntie was out of hearing and when Sharlotte turned back to Maas Mellow, he had vanished into the shadows of the mango tree.

Sharlotte set off at a gallop and caught up with Martha at the bottom of the lane leading towards her house, who enquired where she had been.

[1] "Mi jus see Duppy Mellow," and she told the story of the mango picking ballet dancer. Martha said [2] "Weh mek yu nebber cum mash mi big toa?" Mashing or standing on one's big toe was a magical device and could be used if two people were together and one could see the duppy and the other one did not have that experience. The gifted one could just stamp on the companion's toes, then the latter would also see the duppy.

[3] "Mi cuddn, caas yu gaan lef me."

Arriving at Sharlotte's yard, they turned right into the land where the mango trees grew and they gathered in the fruit, collecting just enough to carry on their heads, a basket each.

Making their way to the house they decided not to wake Sarah, so to while away the time Martha and Sharlotte sat in the kitchen talking, Martha smoking her pipe.

At the first glimmer of daybreak, they made some breakfast, then set off for Kendal, where they found a good location on the forecourt of a shopping piazza, arranged their mangoes and waited for some customers.

They had been doing good business when a man in a brown shirt, black pants, black shoes and carrying a *creng-creng* basket approached Martha, bent over to pick up a ripe mango, placed it carefully in his basket, spun around three times and ..... vanished.

[4] "Mi no ab fi mash yu big toa, dis ya time." said Sharlotte.

---

[1] "I've just seen Duppy Mellow."
[2] "Why didn't you come and stamp on my big toe?"
[3] " I couldn't because you went and left me."
[4] "I've no need to stamp on your big toe this time."

Trick and a Treat

This is the second mischievous story told to me by 'Spoogy'.

****

When I was a boy, my friend and I would often play tricks to frighten people. Of course an easy way to do this was to lie in waiting in the bushes for the little girls to walk by on their way home from school, when we would shake and rustle the undergrowth making low moaning noises. Sometimes they would take to their heels, emitting girlish squeals, but more often we were disappointed to hear them say:

[1] "Cum out, wi noa a yu, Spoogy."

Such pranks lost their interest after a while, so one night we got our heads together to see if we could cook up a better plot. Frightening little girls from the bushes was one thing, but could we play a good trick to frighten the grown-ups we wondered? I was well aware that mamma and pappa were both anxious about being met by a duppy on the lane at night, so I felt that if only we could exploit this fear, we might have the making of a good trick.

I can't remember which one of us came up with the idea, but before we went our different ways that night, we had managed to put together a real winner. He was to come to my yard the following evening when we were to put our fiendish plot into action.

To make our trick work we required good clear moonlight, so that evening couldn't have been better, as the sky was free of clouds and the moon was nearly full.

---

[1] "Come out, we know it's you, Spoogy."

On this particular day of the week, my folks were in the habit of going off down the lane to the shops and would be away long enough for us to implement our plan. I often went with them, but this time I made some excuse or other. I think I told them I'd had a busy day and wanted an early night in bed, so off they went thinking that I was at home safe from trouble. I could predict that it would be quite late when they came back, because they usually couldn't resist stopping at a yard or two to chat and gossip with friends.

We prepared our fiendish little game. Searching in the kitchen, we found a packet of flour, then sat on the porch until the time was ripe, because we didn't want someone else to come on by and spoil our scheme.

The time came when mamma and pappa would soon be home, so picking up the flour we set off down the road to meet them, looking for a suitable spot for the ambush, a place that was dark and deserted, with just one place on the road that was bathed in moonlight shining down through a gap in the trees.

[2] "Mek wi do it ya so!" said Lance, my mate.

"Perfect spot," thought I, pointing at the place where the crime should take place.

Lance lay down, spread eagled right where the shafts of light from the moon were most bright. He lay as though nailed to a cross, but with his legs wide apart. Then I started with the flour, first at the head, sprinkling it very carefully around, then moving down the right side marking out his shoulder, then all around his arm, down his side, around the right leg and so on up the left side back to his head. Now he was completely surrounded by flour.

With great care, so as not to disturb my handy-work, Lance rose to his feet and came to stand beside me and we both gave a grunt of approval at the work of art. There in the middle of the road was the perfect shape of a man surrounded by a halo of white, that seemed to shimmer in the light of the moon. Perfect indeed and just in the nick of time, for from further down the lane we could hear approaching footsteps. With no delay we quickly

---

[2] "Let's do it here."

ducked into the thick undergrowth skirting the lane. We didn't have long to wait.

Around the bend in the road came my parents. Their conversation came to an abrupt end as our flour duppy came into view. Both of them gasped and took a step backwards.

[3] "A wah dat ina de road?"

And there they stood not knowing whether to go back or advance on the duppy. Each time they moved towards the man lying on the road the more the moonlight illuminated the flour to enhance the ghostly apparition.

We could hardly contain ourselves and when Lance started to snigger we both had to retreat for fear of discovery. Moving through the bush until we were clear of the frightened family, we came out onto the road and ran pell mell back to my house. Lance bid me a quick goodnight, then continued running to his own yard. I was well settled in bed before the master of the house and his good lady arrived home a good hour later.

The following morning at breakfast, I enquired whether they had enjoyed their walk to the shops the previous evening and why they had been so late coming back, but I was only greeted by a stony silence.

****

At the next committee meeting of the Lance and Spoogy mischief society, the agenda was disturbed by much laughter and backslapping. It had been a successful wheeze and it needed to be savoured, but when things settled down we eventually came to 'any other business' and made the decision there and then to try out our deception on other victims.

We chose Mr. and Mrs. Johnstone who lived three properties further up the lane from my house. For two whole weeks we 'cased their joint,' getting to know the routines and patterns of movement of the Johnstone household, until our plan of campaign was well formed.

---

[3] "What's that on the road?"

Every Tuesday evening Mr and Mrs. J, would go to a Bible and prayer meeting down the lane at their church and you could set your clock by the starting out and returning from their supplications.

Lance and I sat on the veranda and waved to them as they passed by, heading down hill.

Half an hour before we knew that the prayer meeting would be over we set off, flour in hand, to the scene of our previous hair-raiser, settling down to make our flour duppy. Soon the image lay on the road as before, shimmering hazy white in the beams of moonlight.

Footsteps could be heard, so into the bush we went to settle down for the show. As anticipated, the Johnstones were right on time, but what we hadn't planned for was that they were in the company of half a dozen more church friends. All the better!

As they turned the bend, they were face to face with our apparition and what a disturbance broke out. Two of the ladies screamed out loud. One husband took his wife by the arm, turned straight around and marched off back down the lane waving his Bible in the air. Another man dropped to his knees, raising his arms to heaven, appealing for some divine intervention on his behalf.

Lance and I held on to each other in sheer delight as we witnessed the success of our mission. A melee broke out as our neighbours pushed and pulled at each other, each trying to be at the back of the group and furthest away from our ghost of a man.

Now to operate part two of the plan!

Slipping away we quickly ran up the road to the Johnstone residence, then around the back to climb in an open window into the kitchen. We rummaged through the cupboards and sideboards to find the items needed for the 'scam.'

We put a clean white lace cloth on the dining room table, then put out two placings of plates, knives, forks and spoons. We filled a jug with juice and put two tumblers by its side. Then into the pantry for food to put on the plates and serving dish, taking the occasional bite to make it look as though a meal was under way. When we were satisfied with our masterpiece, we left through

Trick or Treat

the window and raced back to the confused scene taking place before our scary man.

[4] "Maas Johnstone," I cried, "smady a rattle de pot dem ina yu yard."

This piece of information was of enough concern to cause our neighbour to take hold of his wife's hand, scuttle around our duppy and run all the way to his yard, towing his protesting lady behind him.

Leaving his wife on the road, he ran up the porch steps, quickly unlocked the door and charged into the house shouting and bellowing to frighten off any intruder.

Lance and I, of course, had run home with them not wishing to miss the fun, so we stood by the wife on the road, pretending to console her.

Everything was still and quiet inside the house.

A loud wail broke the silence and Mr. Johnstone cried out:

[5] "Lawd a massi, de duppy dem play up ina de food."

Mrs. Johnstone raised her hands to the skies and started to pray.

Meanwhile my friend and I strolled home well pleased with the night's work, busily planning our next exploit with our friend, the flour duppy.

Surely this was infinitely better than frightening little school girls!

---

[4] "Mr. Johnstone, someone is rattling pots in your house."
[5] "Lord have mercy, the duppies have been playing with our food."

Crocodile Man

This story introduces us to some interesting aspects of supernatural beliefs in Jamaica.

Many people hold that some of the creatures that are indigenous to the island have magical powers and are used by the Obeah men and women to carry out unpleasant missions.

The crocodile is attributed with the ability to dress in human clothes and become a debt collector.

The scavenger bird John Crow and the bullfrog often turn up during court cases to divert the course of justice.

This story as told by Winnie and Bibby is based on actual events.

****

Mary was a hard working higgler who sold her products wherever there was business in the Manchester and Clarendon districts of Jamaica. She had built up a good reputation by selling good fried fish at various venues around the area.

What she would do, would be to travel regularly down through May Pen to Old Harbour Bay, where she would haggle with a fisherman for a good buy of fresh fish. Taking them home she would lovingly spice them up and fry them, after which tasks she could then sell them cold to her many regular customers at surrounding markets.

In the first instance, she had only been able to get this enterprise off the ground due to the kind but wily help of an Old Harbour man of the sea. She had been outlining her plan to him, when he proposed to her that he would stake her the money to get her venture under way. She would take fish from him with an 'I owe you,' would cook them up, would sell them to her customers and then pay him when next she collected a new supply of fish. This arrangement had been working well for many, many months, but was always conditional that her debt was paid up with each new consignment.

It was the breaking of this promise that started all the bother, and set off a chain of horrendous events.

****

Ruffus Anderson was having a party in his yard and had invited a number of friends to visit him for food, drinks and some dancing, so he had made prior order with Mary for some of her delicious fried fish, for she had come highly recommended.

Mary took his order and made the necessary arrangements with her colleague at Old Harbour to increase the size of her usual collection, so all was going well.

The fish were duly spiced, cooked and taken to Ruffus, who thanked our higgler and informed her that he would pay her the following morning. This took Mary aback somewhat, because she was expecting cash on delivery, but no amount of arguing would change his decision.

Mary duly called the following morning as requested, to find her customer had gone out. She called again later but to no avail. This she did daily for a week, but Ruffus was either out or gave some excuse like not having time to go to the bank. You know how it goes!

Well! the time came for her visit to Old Harbour, but Mr. Anderson was still in her debt, so she had no other recourse but to place her problem in the hands of the fisherman. He frowned at first, but as Mary did not normally renege on her deals, he agreed to let the matter ride for another week. Another week went by and still no money was forthcoming, so our fisherman was less reasonable to hear of the continuing dilemma. He was prepared to let things go for yet another seven days, but really laid down the law and warned of dire consequences if the money was not in his hands by the next visit.

We know by now that Ruffus had no intention of paying off his debt, but when Mary tried to blame him for cheating her, the Old Harbour man said:

[1] "Mi no ca a fi who fault! Mi waan mi moni! If mi no get pay, yu wi si w'appen to oonoo."

Three weeks passed and he let the matter ride, but when a month was up he closed her account.

By this time the story had spread around the bay workers that Mary's credit was no good and she was unable to strike up another deal. Her fish frying days were over!!

****

The fisherman stood before the house of the local Obeah man.

It was his first visit and he could not shake off the anxiety that was overwhelming him. He could not put his finger on it but just standing in the yard gave him the shivers.

[2] "Comeen fren! Wah yu waan?"

Joseph mustered a faint smile from somewhere, then followed the Obeah man into his house, where he was invited to sit in the living room. He looked around. To his surprise it was just an everyday living room. Quite ordinary really.

He had expected to be taken into some ominous place, littered with amulets and charm bracelets that sat on altars with black candles surrounded by implements of magic.

In a way he was a little disappointed.

He coughed, then explained the reason for his visit, requesting whether anything could be done about Mary's bad debt and the troublesome Ruffus Anderson.

****

---

[1] "I don't care who's fault it is! I want my money! If I don't get paid, you will see what will happen to the two of you."

[2] "Come in friend! What do you want?"

Aunt Sarah was a teenager at this time and Mamma had sent her off down to Maas Chang's shop. He was a Chinese man. Coming up the road to meet her was a tall figure, dressed in a top hat, a long black coat with tails and black trousers to match. He wore a white shirt, black tie and shiny black shoes. He looked very much like an undertaker.

[3] "Evlink Miss," he said in a strange watery thin voice. "Yu noa whe Mr. Andison live?"

Sarah averted her eyes and shook her head.

She knew exactly where Ruffus lived, but she was responding to the counsel of her parents, who told her to be wary of strangers and not to get the neighbours into trouble by being too hasty with information. Turning quickly on her heels, Sarah returned to her mission, running down to the store to buy the few items that her mother required to make pappa's dinner that evening.

Half an hour later she was back home, so leaving the purchase and the change in the kitchen, she called out that she was just going up the road to see her friend.

Up the lane, she had to pass Maas Anderson's place and there he was, the man in black, just walking from the gate to Ruffus's front door. Her curiosity aroused, Sarah stopped at the gate to watch this stranger waddle up the drive. How could it be? The man had a long black tail with a knobbly ridge running to its tip hanging down beneath his coat tails, that 'swished' from side to side as he ambled to the house.

Taking fright, Sarah ran swiftly back home, to blurt out to her mother about her strange encounter that evening.

[4] "Lawd amassi, de crocodile man cum fi collec' a det."

****

Crocodile man knocked on the door, and Ruffus was quick to answer.

---

[3] "Evening Miss! Do you know where Mr. Anderson lives?"
[4] "Lord have mercy, the crocodile man has come to collect a debt."

[5] "Evlink sir, wha yu waan mi to du fi yu?" said Ruffus.

(Strange, isn't it, that the crocodile man is never recognised as a reptile until his tail is seen from behind!)

Crocodile man explained to Ruffus that he had been sent by the Obeah man in Old Harbour to collect the debt on behalf of the fisherman.

[6] "Mi naa ab no moni fi pay yu. So cum out a mi warra warra yard. Guh weh!"

The debt collector took a step back from the door and speaking with a hiss in his voice he replied:

[7] "Yu a go sorry," and spinning around he headed off down the road.

****

The following week Ruffus began to behave strangely.

He started to regularly go late for work, and the foreman had to pass comment on his appearance, as he often left home unwashed and unshaven. He was seen in the lane, standing quite still, gazing into heaven and holding conversations with unseen persecutors, whom he cursed and requested that they leave him alone. He verbally abused his neighbours, accusing them of all sorts of conspiracies to do him harm.

The crocodile man's curse was taking effect. Ruffus was going mad!

****

Mary was getting back on her feet, having taken to fruit and vegetable higgling at the market. She was selling coconuts this day when who should come her way but Ruffus Anderson. He had been prowling around the market stalls, tormenting and

---

[5] "Evening Sir, what can I do for you?"
[6] "I have no money to pay you. So come out of my b..... (swearing) yard. Go away!"
[7] "You're going to be sorry."

cussing at the sellers, who would take so much then drive him away with well directed missiles, using anything that came to hand. Ruffus came to Mary's stall and stood for a while, looking her up and down, grimacing and gesticulating from time to time. She tried to ignore him.

[8] "Gi mi waan jelly!" mumbled Ruffus.

[9] "Ruffus Andison, yu still hooa mi fi di fish dem! Noa moni noa jelly."

Ruffus dug his hand deep into his dirty torn pants and just found enough for the purchase, handed it over and took the coconut from the stall, then just stood facing Mary as though the transaction was incomplete.

[10] "Wah else yu waan?"

[11] "Chop mi jelly!"

[12] "Si de cutliss deh, chop it yusef."

Ruffus stood silent for a moment, then slowly bent down to pick up the machete. He stared at this broad heavy knife, raised it high in the air, then brought it down in a broad curving swing to chop Mary's head clean from her shoulders. Whatever she might have said to Ruffus would now never leave her lips, as her head rolled down the aisle between the stalls and the screaming higglers.

Ruffus stood laughing maniacally, bathed with the blood pumping from the neck of the corpse, that still sat upright in the chair. Then he went berserk, rushing around the market, clearing all in his path, everyone rushing out of his way until turning a corner he came face to face with a man. A tall figure of a man dressed in a top hat, a long black coat with tails and black trousers to match. He wore a white shirt, a black tie and shiny black shoes. We know now that it wasn't an undertaker!

---

[8] "Give me a coconut!"

[9] "Ruffus Anderson, you still owe me for the fish. You'll get no coconuts without money."

[10] "What else do you want?"

[11] "Cut my coconut!"

[12] "See the cutlass there? Cut it yourself."

Crocodile Man

Ruffus stopped dead in his tracks. Dropping the machete, he raised his arms appealingly to the crocodile man, falling to his knees, begging for mercy and wailing most pitifully.

Crocodile man pointed to Mary's head saying:

[13] "De full debt pay now!"

****

Rufus the lunatic was carried off to an asylum where he remained for many a year. When he was released home, he died suddenly of causes unknown. It was rumoured that Mary's family had their revenge by poisoning him.

Whenever this tale is told, outstanding debts are PROMPTLY paid.

---

[13] "The debt is now fully paid."

About the Author

David Brailsford was born in Nottingham, England in 1930. He was educated at the High Pavement Grammar School. He qualified as a Psychiatric Nurse in 1955 and progressed through his profession to be a Senior Nursing Officer. He developed a Staff in-house Training Department and worked with clients as a Registered Drama therapist.

He is now retired and spends much of his time writing tales of folk lore and fantasy.

He has three daughters and ten grandchildren. He lives with his Jamaican-born wife in Nottingham, but loves to spend as much time as he can in his second 'home', Jamaica.

About the Illustrator

John Stilgoe was born in Liverpool, England in 1956.

He earned a BA (Hons) degree at North Staffordshire Polytechnic in 1978. In 1979 he was awarded P.G.C.E. and A.T.D. teaching qualifications. Since then he has taught Art and Technology in colleges and secondary schools throughout England and is now Head of Art, Design and Technology at Mount Grace High School, Hinckley.

His cartoons and illustrations have appeared in magazines and posters; many of the originals are now in private collections.

He is happily married with three sons and three daughters who share his interest in art.

Printed in the United States
24059LVS00003B/1-96